GAUTAM S. MENGLE

INTERSECTIONS

First published by Westland Publications Private Limited, in association with Golden Pen, in 2020

1st Floor, A Block, East Wing, Plot No. 40, SP Infocity, Dr MGR Salai, Perungudi, Kandanchavadi, Chennai 600096

Westland and the Westland logo are the trademarks of Westland Publications Private Limited, or its affiliates.

Copyright © Gautam S. Mengle, 2020

ISBN: 9789389648478

10 9 8 7 6 5 4 3 2 1

This is a work of fiction. Names, characters, organisations, places, events and incidents are either products of the author's imagination or used fictitiously.

All rights reserved

Typeset by SÜRYA, New Delhi
Printed at Manipal Technologies Limited, Manipal

No part of this book may be reproduced, or stored in a retrieval system, or transmitted in any form or by any means, electronic, mechanical, photocopying, recording, or otherwise, without express written permission of the publisher.

INTERSECTIONS

Gautam S. Mengle has been a journalist on the crime beat for eleven years and counting, and has worked across newspapers during this time. He joined *The Asian Age* as a trainee reporter in September 2008, and within two months was thrown into the biggest story of the year — the 26/11 terror attacks, an experience which went a long way in shaping him as a crime reporter. It was also during his four-year stint with *The Asian Age* that he worked under S. Hussain Zaidi, who was then the Resident Editor, and went on to assist him on some of his books in a minor capacity. From *The Asian Age*, he moved on to *The Indian Express* in 2012 and then to *The Hindu* in 2015 to be part of the pilot team for its Mumbai edition.

Fiction writing has been a hobby since his teenage years.

Gautam took up stand-up comedy as a hobby in August 2018 and has performed at enough open mics to be able to identify as at least a part-time, if not struggling, stand-up comic. Other hobbies include mentoring journalism interns, sly-tweeting about them and calling out sexist jokes on social media platforms.

You can find him on Twitter @NotMengele

For my mother, Shubha
Without her, there would be nothing

Prologue

She could smell his breath.

It smelt the same every time. A disgusting mixture of cigarettes, cheap rum and garlic that made her want to throw up as he shoved his face in the crook of her neck.

As she struggled, he roughly shoved her against the wall from behind, and she could feel the ridges in the wall's surface digging into the skin of her cheek. Using one forearm to keep her pinned, he used his other hand to raise the hem of her skirt.

She fought hard to not let the panic and pain cloud her senses, and did her best to focus on escaping. She could feel his hand on her thigh, and her nausea felt stronger than ever.

Blindly, she flailed out behind her, her elbow glancing off his cheekbone, and he threw her to the floor with a muted curse. She used her hands to break her fall, ignoring the pain in her forearms, and tried to crawl away, just as he caught both her legs and pulled her towards him. As her palms dragged against the ground, one of them touched something hard and cold, and she instinctively closed her fingers around it.

As he tried to turn her around on her back, she saw she was holding a broken bottle, the jagged edge glinting in the stray neon lights of the night outside. Without thinking, without hesitation, she let only her instinct to survive take over. As he finally succeeded in turning her around, she pushed the knife-like edge towards him with all the force she could muster.

She woke up just as it pierced his throat and the blood sprayed all over her face.

The dream wasn't a new one. She gave herself a minute to let her breathing come back to normal before she realised it. Even though it was night in her dream, as it always had been, the air was hotter than it usually was.

The last cobwebs of sleep cleared away and she quickly sat up in her bed. It took her only two seconds to spot it.

The corridor outside her hotel room was on fire.

1

People often talk about the beauty of south Mumbai. The pre-Independence era architecture of several of its buildings, the arches and pillars of the Chhatrapati Shivaji Terminus Railway Station, the regal façade of the Brihanmumbai Municipal Corporation building when it's all lit up at night, and countless other aspects, have been the subject of many a coffee-table book.

Funny, Assistant Police Inspector Uday Mhatre thought, as he sat in the police vehicle, engine idling, waiting for the signal to change. *No one seems to have noticed how ugly it also is. Or maybe they just ignore that.*

A teeming mass of humanity surged against Mhatre's police SUV as he waited with thinly veiled impatience. Men and women of all ages pressed past, engulfing him, making him want to draw his service weapon and start shooting blindly into the crowd. He hated this hour, when the office-goers were released from their corporate prisons and made a mad dash for the first train or bus home. Some talking, some shouting, some laughing, some pissing him off by simply sweating so much that he wanted to grab them and beat them till they begged for mercy.

Add to that the chaos of the buses and the myriad cars and two-wheelers, and Mhatre was pretty sure someone was going to throw a couple of live grenades into the office rush one evening out of sheer frustration.

Mhatre shook his head hard a couple of times. He wasn't just irritated at the city. The previous night had, like too many nights before, been filled with more liquor than was good for him, and as his system struggled to process the alcohol, there was a dull ache in his head.

The signal finally turned green and he drove ahead, pausing only to snarl at a biker who wouldn't stop honking, and pulled up outside DCP Samad Khan's office within five minutes. The drive from Colaba to CST had taken him forty-five minutes, thanks to the traffic. Parking the vehicle along the pavement, he quickly entered and took the stairs two at a time till he reached Khan's cabin on the first floor. An orderly, who was expecting him, ushered him into a waiting room. Ten minutes later, he was summoned inside.

Mhatre paused outside to make sure his shirt was properly tucked in and the top button, usually left undone, was fastened. His posting with a special squad that operated from the Colaba Police Station compound did not require him to be in uniform. He nodded at the orderly, who held the door for him, and stepped in, directly in front of Khan.

'Sit,' was all Khan said, without looking up from the file he was reading, as Mhatre came smartly to attention and clicked his heels.

Mhatre sat in one of the plush chairs.

Khan looked up and regarded him in silence for a second as he slowly shut the file and slid it aside.

'You do know why you're here, Mhatre?' Khan asked.

Mhatre said nothing.

'I asked you a question,' Khan said sharply.

'I was told you wanted to see me, sir,' Mhatre replied.

Khan leaned forward in his seat. He had, only two months earlier, taken over as DCP of the upmarket south Mumbai, or SoBo, area, designated 'Zone I' for policing purposes. Already there were whispers about him making changes and doing away with 'undesirable elements'.

Although Mhatre wasn't sure if he was an undesirable element—yet—he wouldn't have been surprised if he found himself on Khan's radar. *God knows I've given him enough reason*, he thought.

'I understand politics,' Khan began, and Mhatre nodded to himself inwardly.

Definitely on his radar, he thought to himself.

'I understand the need to appease vote banks and the necessity of playing to the gallery,' Khan went on. 'And I am aware of the fact that certain things need to be tolerated so that other things can be dealt with.'

Mhatre waited for the axe to fall.

'But, Mr Mhatre,' Khan said, leaning forward in his seat, 'what *you* need to understand is that there are rules, and there are limits. The adjustment for the sake of the vote banks works both ways, and cannot be pulled off if all parties concerned do not play their role.'

Here it comes, Mhatre thought.

'For example, I understand the need to keep a decorated officer in a plum posting so that the vote banks who regard him as their hero are kept happy enough to vote the same government in, in the coming term. But you need to understand that if your conduct does not change, I will see to it that you're transferred to Local Arms, and that you stay there till they kick me off the bloody force.'

Mhatre had heard about Khan long before he met him. A no-nonsense IPS officer from a family of IPS and IAS officers, Khan was famous — or infamous, depending on who was describing him — for not bowing down to political pressure beyond a point. He was willing to go along with the whims and fancies of the ruling government as long as it did not interfere with his primary mission, which, according to everyone who knew Khan, was basic old-fashioned policing. While he was not exactly a stickler for rules, he had no patience with games.

What made Khan formidable was that he had a lot of friends in the news media. In general, honest and upright cops tend to shy away from the media, not wanting to get caught up in controversies. Khan made it a point to make friends among journalists wherever he went so that every time a politician strayed from the straight and narrow, he would leak information about their dirty games to the press, making sure it was never traced back to him.

'Do you understand?' Khan asked sharply.

Mhatre nodded. 'Yes, sir,' he said.

'Are you sure?'

'Yes, sir.'

'Then tell me why you have illegally detained three men in the Colaba Police Station lock-up,' Khan said abruptly.

For them, Mhatre thought. *For Shireen, Reema, Sehar, Vasant and Ashok.*

'I have not, sir,' he said aloud.

Khan, who was at that moment sipping water from a glass, almost spat it out. He put his glass down and glared.

'Explain,' was all he could say.

'I released them an hour ago after questioning them, sir,' Mhatre said, keeping his face deadpan.

Realisation dawned on Khan's face, and so did rage. The law dictates that anyone detained by the police should either be released within twenty-four hours or placed under arrest and produced before a magistrate court. Mhatre had released the three suspects exactly twenty-three hours and thirty minutes after he had detained them. Therefore, it wasn't, strictly speaking, an illegal detention. It was perfectly within the ambit of the law.

'I'll expect a full report by tomorrow morning,' Khan said quietly.

'Yes, sir.'

'Get out.'

Mhatre stood up, saluted and walked out of the office. Quickly, he made his way to his SUV, slid into the driver's seat and sat silent for a minute, the back of his head resting against the seat.

Then he fished his cellphone out of his pocket, accessed the photo gallery and scrolled through five photographs in quick succession on the screen.

I need a drink, he thought, placing the cellphone on the dashboard and turning on the ignition.

2

Mhatre had just started the ignition and was about to pull into the traffic outside Khan's office when his wireless crackled.

'Fire at Sitaara Hotel, Kabootar Khana Circle. People trapped. Repeat, people trapped inside.'

Mhatre was part of a special squad that reported directly to Khan and only handled special cases. Strictly speaking, he was not required to respond to any old call about what was probably a minor blaze in a largely unknown hotel.

Protocol, however, also dictated that every nearby policeman respond to an ongoing emergency and Kabootar Khana Circle was a stone's throw from Khan's office.

What the hell, Mhatre thought. He could use the brownie points with Khan. Besides, the action at his favourite bar, to where he'd been headed, wouldn't begin till a couple of hours later, and he had no one to go home early to.

'API Mhatre, Zone I Squad. I'm five minutes away,' he said into his wireless, hoping Khan was listening, and turned on his siren. Despite its urgent alarm and lights, pedestrians and motorists still took their time to make way for him as he took a U-turn.

'*Abey, hatt na!*' he bellowed at a teenager on a bicycle, who almost fell off his ride in fright. The first of the fire engines from the Colaba Fire Station pulled up behind him, its siren shrieking as well. He looked in the rear-view mirror and stuck one hand out of his window in a slight wave.

I'll make way, hang on, the unspoken message said.

The driver of the fire tender returned the gesture with an urgent wave of his own.

Hurry, he meant.

Sirens screaming, both vehicles sped to Kabootar Khana Circle, which was just two lanes away, and took a right turn to see the flames billowing out of as many as five windows of the top floor of the hotel. It was a modest four-storey affair, one of the many three- to four-storey buildings on that street. It was a bustling commercial area, with a wide range of establishments in each building. Mhatre guessed that the ground floor had the reception and the kitchen, while the upper floors had the rooms.

Mhatre parked his SUV horizontally right in the middle of the lane and the fire tender followed suit around a hundred metres ahead, effectively blocking traffic. Mhatre and the firemen got out of their vehicles at the same time and met each other midway, just as three constables came running up.

'How bad, do you think?' Mhatre asked the fire officer who was clearly in charge.

'That? A nightmare. Single access point, closely packed rooms and people trapped inside. I'm escalating the call to Level III,' the fire officer said, reaching for his wireless radio.

All emergencies, like fires or building collapses, were graded from Level I to Level V, with Level V being the most serious. Level III was dangerously in the middle and the firefighters would need all the help they could get.

Mhatre unclipped his own wireless from his belt.

'API Mhatre, Zone I Squad. Sitaara Hotel fire is now Level III. Repeat, fire call is now Level III.'

'Copy, Mhatre,' Khan himself replied before the control room could acknowledge him. 'I'm on my way. Zone I staff, respond fast.'

As Khan's command was met with a flurry of acknowledgements, Mhatre remembered what his instructors had told him and his batchmates back at the Maharashtra Police Academy in Nashik.

A policeman is always the first responder to any emergency. Everyone else gets there later. You might have entered the force with dreams of catching dreaded criminals and winning medals, but what you do in times of everyday emergencies will always go a long way in adding to your track record. You don't get to choose the scene of action. You just need to act.

Let's act, Mhatre thought, as he plunged into the crowd of civilians and started pushing them back with the constables' help. With the fire brigade now on the spot, the police's first priority was crowd control. They had to make sure the fire brigade had unhindered access to the site of the emergency, and that meant clearing away all the civilians to a safe distance.

Even as he was working, Mhatre watched a well-oiled system fall smoothly into place around him. Barricades were rushed in from the Azad Maidan, which wasn't far away, on a truck and quickly unloaded at the site, with DCP Khan himself supervising. The Azad Maidan, being the venue of choice for all protests in the city, always had an abundance of police barricades lying around.

Mhatre tossed his car keys to a constable, who ran to the vehicle and drove it away, letting the barricades cordon off the lane. The fire engine stayed where it was, strategically well placed.

Across the street, well away from the reach of any falling embers or burning debris, an enclosure was created out of police barricades for journalists, who had started arriving by then. Mhatre personally herded all of them inside the enclosure, ensuring they had enough space to set up their cameras and other equipment.

'Kya, Mhatre sir!' one of them called out. 'You here?'

Mhatre, thanks to an episode at the very start of his career, was something of a 'media darling', a tag that refused to go away. Mhatre just grinned at the reporter and turned back to the task at hand.

More fire tenders came speeding up to the spot and soon the entire street was closed off. No one realised when, but a squad of white uniformed traffic police personnel reached the scene to divert motorists to alternative routes.

Ambulances arrived speedily and a path was cleared for them. The firemen would escort the survivors, coughing or wheezing or nursing burn injuries, outside the building, where the cops and paramedics would take charge of them, while the firemen rushed back inside.

At the same time, two strong hoses sprayed massive amounts of water at the fire, containing it to the top floor.

Bang in the middle of the operation, a man in his fifties broke through the crowd of bystanders and tried to get past the barricades, tears streaming from both his eyes. Mhatre went running to him and tried to push him back.

'That's my hotel!' the man bawled. 'That's my livelihood!'

Mhatre made a judgement call.

'Let him through,' he told the constable manning the barricade. 'Not you, fuckers!' he snapped at two others who also tried to slip in. They cowered before his anger and backed away.

Mhatre led the owner of Sitaara Hotel, Hirenbhai Goswami, to the pavement directly in front of the building and made him sit down, crouching down beside him. The man finally stopped crying and took a few deep breaths, trying hard not to break down again.

'Should I get you some water?' Mhatre asked.

Goswami shook his head and stared with glassy eyes up at the floors on fire.

'I was renovating the place,' he said, so softly that Mhatre missed the words.

'What did you say?' Mhatre asked.

'I finally started renovating it. I was having the top floor repainted and repaired. That bastard contractor wanted to use gas cutters to cut out the old metal doors. That's what must have caused it.'

Alarms went off in Mhatre's brain.

'There is flammable material on the top floor!' he yelled into his wireless. 'Paint, thinner and gas cutters. Repeat, flammable material on the top floor!'

Some firemen on the ground floor heard him even as the control room flashed the information around. The firemen relayed it to their colleagues on their own wireless network. Within minutes, those who had entered the building were recalled. The fire officer in charge quickly decided that, unless there was a definite indication of more people being trapped inside, no fireman would enter till the flames were completely doused.

'You saved us there,' he said to Mhatre gratefully. Mhatre waved away his thanks and looked at his watch. An hour and a half had passed.

It took another half-hour for the fire brigade to declare that things were under control. Then they entered the building to finish cooling operations. They advanced slowly and carefully. A single residual spark could come into contact with something combustible and start the fire again.

Mhatre and Khan converged at the entrance at the same time, after giving the firemen a five-minute lead. Mhatre stopped when he saw Khan was going the same way and let him pass first, as protocol dictated. Khan went straight for the reception desk and found the guest register.

'How many did we rescue?' Khan called out, going through the details.

'Took six out of here!' a fireman answered from somewhere.

Khan scanned through the register.

'Five rooms occupied. Three couples and two singles,' he said. 'Get the owner in here.'

Another fireman came up to them.

'We found the manager on the staircase to the top floor. He suffocated to death in the smoke,' he said matter-of-factly.

Both cops shook their heads in silence. Both of them had seen too much death on the job to repeat the same banalities.

'The rest of the staff made it out safely,' the fireman added, before heading back up.

Over the next twenty minutes, with the owner's help, they confirmed that both the singles and two of the three couples registered as guests had been rescued by the fire brigade. That left one couple unaccounted for.

'One more body!' someone called out. 'Male, forties. Burned pretty badly. Inside one of the rooms.'

Mhatre went over to the base of the stairs where a couple of firemen were standing.

'Anyone else?' Mhatre called out. The question was relayed to the top floor and the reply came back within the minute. There was no one else inside, dead or alive.

Mhatre took a step back, thinking hard.

'Something wrong?' the hotel owner asked, looking at Mhatre who said nothing but turned around and walked to the door. The owner and Khan followed him curiously.

Standing in the hotel's doorway, Mhatre slowly ran his eyes over the crowds gathered beyond the barricades.

Intersections

'If the man, out of the third couple, is lying dead up there,' he finally said, 'where is the woman? Why is she not fighting to get through the crowds, screaming her head off, asking about her partner?'

3

'Isn't it beautiful?' she said softly.

Lying on the sand, with his head in her lap and her fingers in his hair, he had to agree; the sun was slowly sinking in the distance, and the sky was turning a beautiful mélange of colours.

'Beyond beautiful,' he said, looking directly up at her.

She knew what he meant.

'I was talking about the sunset,' she said, gently tapping his forehead.

He raised himself and turned around to face her.

'And I meant ... this. Us.'

She smiled.

They were at their favourite spot on the beach, watching the waves crash against the shore while the wind blew past them. It was getting late, but people still milled around. Couples holding hands. Children running about. Old men and women taking leisurely walks. Policemen patrolling the beach. Everyone kept to their own companions. Everyone valued their own privacy, even out in the open, on a semi-crowded beach.

Every so often, however, people passing by would slow down to stare at the young lovers. He didn't blame them. They wouldn't understand.

He knew this when they had started their rather forbidden journey three months ago. They had sat down together on a bench in a deserted classroom in his college after classes were done and had a long conversation. She had been full of doubts, as he had known she would. He, however, had been completely sure of this. He still was.

'People will talk,' she said. 'They will say all sorts of things. Call me all sorts of names.'

'I won't let them, he told her. 'I won't let anyone say a single word about you. I will kill anyone who does.'

She reached out and placed her fingers on his lips.

'Don't,' was all she said.

She let her fingers stay on his lips for a few seconds before letting her hand fall away.

'Look,' he said. 'I get it. You're older than me by a few years ...'

'Twelve years, Rohit,' she corrected him gently. 'You're sixteen. I'm twenty-eight. And I'm your teacher. This is just wrong.'

He took her hand in his.

'Then why doesn't it feel wrong to me?' he asked.

She said nothing, just closed her hand over his.

'Does it to you?' he pressed. 'Does it feel wrong to you?'

Very slowly, she shook her head.

'I'm just not sure about this ...'she began.

'I am,' he said. 'If there is one thing I am sure of, it is that I love you.'

She looked into his eyes and she saw he meant it. And just like that, their romance began.

It took some effort but she managed to convince him to keep their relationship a secret for the time being. In the end, he agreed, just to keep her happy. He actually wanted to shout it out from every rooftop in the city. For the first time, he had got something he actually wished for. He felt he deserved to go to town about it, just so that he could see the jealous faces of all those people who thought so little of him. His father, his classmates, other teachers. He wanted to rub it in everyone's face that, whatever they thought of him, he loved someone and that someone loved him back.

His father, in particular. His alcoholic, wife-beating, abusive father who spent his days telling his son he was worthless, and nights getting drunk and hitting his mother over the years till she finally slipped out of the house one night. They found her on the railway tracks the next morning. The motorman of the train, in an informal conversation, told the investigating officer that she had stood by the tracks, calmly walked into the middle when she saw the train coming and stood there without moving while he madly sounded the horn.

'I think she was smiling,' the motorman said. Standing outside the officer's cabin, Rohit heard everything.

The police, however, after a routine inquiry, made the motorman give a formal statement saying she stumbled and fell while crossing the tracks, and dismissed the case as an accident.

His father reacted to her death in a completely unexpected manner. After they went back home from the crematorium — not that there was too much left of her to cremate — he emptied every bottle of whisky in the house into the toilet before throwing the empties out. Then he went into Rohit's room and sat next to him on his bed for a long time.

Rohit sensed he wanted to say something. But he was simply not interested in what that could be. He sat with his back to his father the entire time till he heard him stand up and leave the room. Then he curled up on the bed and cried bitterly.

'You're thinking of her again?' she said, jolting him back to the present.

'I'm ... I'm so sorry ...' he began, but she shook her head.

'Don't be. It's nothing for you to be sorry about. I just wish I could take your pain away.'

He reached out and ran a hand through her hair. A middle-aged man walking by stared at him.

'You already have, my love,' he said, and they both smiled.

'It's time we leave,' she said.

Reluctantly, he nodded his agreement and they both stood up. They walked hand-in-hand to the main road, where they shared a quick hug. She was uncomfortable with public displays of affection.

Then they parted ways and she went to her scooter while he turned the other way, towards his bicycle. As he heard her scooter start up, he turned back. She waved at him before turning the accelerator, and he stood watching till she took a turn and disappeared.

4

Shireen. Reema. Sehar. Vasant. Ashok.

It was as if the names were permanently etched into Mhatre's brain. They kept repeating themselves in his mind and only faded away when he was drunk enough.

Which was turning out to be every night, Mhatre thought to himself as he stood in the kitchen, waiting for the tea to boil.

After the operation at Kabootar Khana had been completed, Mhatre drove to the Colaba Police Station and parked his SUV in its compound. Then he got onto his bike and drove to his usual bar near Metro Cinema, where he got so drunk that he half passed out in his seat.

The bar manager, who had seen this happen several times before, called a taxi for him, and Mhatre honestly could not remember if he had paid the driver who brought him home.

His head felt as if there was a war going on inside, and his mouth was parched. He poured the tea into a mug and took it to the living room of his two-room flat in the Officers' Quarters in Girgaum.

Sitting down at the small dining table, Mhatre picked up his cellphone and went to the photo gallery once more. The five pictures were in the Favourites folder and he accessed them with a single tap on the screen. Not even his parents' photos were in that folder.

Shireen. Very fair skin, brown hair, brown eyes. She was smiling happily at the camera. The picture had been taken by her father.

Reema. Her smile was a little more guarded. She was self-conscious and not a good poser. Still, this was among her best pictures.

Sehar. The youngest of them all, at five years old. Dressed in a Wonder Woman costume and posing with a goofy look on her face.

Vasant. The oldest, at forty-two. The years showing on his face but the smile still a happy one.

Ashok. Strong-faced. Looking ready to take on the world in his football uniform.

Mhatre put his phone away and finished his tea. The pounding in his head was still there, but he had work to do.

In an hour, he was ready and on his way back to the bar, where he picked up his bike and rode to the Colaba Police Station. His team, led by Police Inspector Sharad Patankar, worked out of a three-room structure in the police station compound. The structure previously used to be a storage space for documents, but after the digitisation of police files began, all hard copies were stored in a central depository in the Mumbai Police headquarters. Ever short of space, like the rest of the city, the department had accommodated the squad in the now vacant structure.

The squad had been formed by Khan's predecessor, DCP Arvind Tamhane, three years previously, when Mhatre was still a sub-inspector. He had been freshly transferred from the Shivaji Park Police Station to Cuffe Parade, and Tamhane had handpicked him for the squad.

It had no name and its members were not required to wear uniforms, as they were not saddled with the police station's daily duties. Tamhane's agenda had been simple. He had had enough of the Crime Branch swooping in and solving high-profile crimes while the police station staff struggled to manage patrolling, bandobast, preventive action and the myriad other duties that hardly left any time for crime detection. The more serious the crime, the longer the investigation took. Scores of suspects had to be questioned, CCTV camera footage examined, call detail records scanned, forensic and medical reports analysed and, based on all of these, the investigating team had to apply its own brains to arrive at solutions.

The Crime Branch, on the other hand, did not have any of the other duties and was formed solely to focus on crime detection. Once the ruling branch of the police department, when the underworld was in its heyday, the Crime Branch now found itself with plenty of free time, and skilled and experienced officers at its disposal. As a result, officers from the local Crime Branch units had started investigating high-profile cases like murders, rapes and armed robberies registered with the police stations in their zone. It pained Tamhane to see the Crime Branch chief wax eloquent about the performances of his officers at press conferences, while his own men struggled with their workload as well as the embarrassment.

Tamhane's squad was tasked with taking up these same cases for investigation — and solving them before the Crime Branch did. As the rules allowed the Crime Branch to conduct parallel investigations into any case, Tamhane couldn't exactly stop them, but he was damned if he wasn't going to beat them at their own game. With time, the squad went from being called 'DCP sir's squad' to simply the Zone I Squad.

The idea worked. With no other duties, the squad started focusing only on serious cases registered in the south Mumbai zone. Patankar, who was himself a veteran of the Crime Branch, patiently guided and coached Mhatre in the methods of investigation. Mhatre's own drive and doggedness helped. The Crime Branch wasn't too pleased, and Tamhane, for exactly this reason, was more than happy.

Intersections

When Khan took over from Tamhane, the first thing he did was to call the squad to his office. Mhatre had been promoted to API by that time but had been retained in his present posting.

'The numbers speak for themselves in terms of the cases you guys have solved. I just want to tell everyone that rules exist for a reason and cannot be bent in the name of getting results. I love a good detection rate, but I also love a good image of the police. The people need to trust us, not fear us,' Khan briefed his squad at the very beginning.

It was the middle of the week and the Colaba Police Station compound was bustling with activity. The same compound also housed the office of the divisional assistant commissioner of police, and there were plenty of visitors waiting to be met.

Mhatre parked his bike at his usual spot and walked into the structure that had become their office. Patankar was already there.

'Heard you stirred up some action at the fire last night?' he said, one eye on the television, which was casting the news.

'Huh?' Mhatre looked blank. He had no idea what his reporting head was talking about.

Patankar kept half-looking at the television.

'Khan called,' he said. 'He wants us to look into this missing woman you wouldn't shut up about.'

Mhatre chuckled. Patankar was known for two things in the police force: exaggerating facts and ruining Bollywood songs by singing the wrong lyrics on purpose. Tales were still told across the department about his rendition of *O Hansini*, in which he replaced *'mere armaanon ke pankh lagaake'* with *'mere armaanon ke laude lagaake'*.

'I just had an idea,' Mhatre said. 'I didn't expect him to take it so seriously.'

'Good idea, though,' Patankar replied. 'If those two were indeed a couple, the woman should have been around. I checked with the hospital and the woman wasn't brought there for sure. Also, nobody's claimed the man's body as yet.'

Mhatre, who was sitting at his desk, looked up at Patankar with interest.

'Curious,' was all he said.

Patankar finally looked away from the television and straightened from his slouching position.

'Chal,' he said, standing up. 'Let's get started.'

Patankar walked into the inner room, which was his own office, and Mhatre followed him in. Patankar opened a window and took out a pack of cigarettes from his pocket. Mhatre did the same. Smoking was officially forbidden in government offices. Which meant that all smokers in government service had to find ways around the rule. A separate structure tucked away at the back of the compound was a boon in this scenario. Patankar's room was the innermost one, and very few people made it that far inside. His subordinates dealt with most visitors.

Intersections

Both the cops lit up and sat down. Quickly, they planned their next steps. Mhatre would see if the CCTV footage of the hotel had escaped the fire and collect the footage if it had. If it hadn't, he would have to put in a request to the control room to submit footage of all state-installed cameras covering the approach roads to the hotel in hopes of identifying the woman.

At the same time, Patankar would send out a request seeking information on any missing person complaint registered for a man, a woman or a couple over the last one week. If that didn't yield results, they would widen the time frame.

Mhatre would also check with the doctors conducting the autopsy to see if they could provide a description of the man's facial features. Most of his body had been badly burned, and his face had been little more than bits of charred flesh hanging off the bone.

'The owner, Goswami, was away for a couple of days. The guest records state that the couple checked in yesterday morning and were going to check out today. Since the owner was not around, the only person who could have seen the woman long enough to identify her would be the manager,' Mhatre said.

'Isn't he dead?' Patankar asked.

Mhatre nodded.

'Speak to the staff too. At least one of them must have seen her.'

'Yes, sir. If there's nothing else, I'll go down to the hotel now.'

'Sure. There's just some paperwork to be done, but I'll get one of the others on it.'

Mhatre stood up, saluted and turned to go.

Patankar settled back in his chair and started singing in a low voice.

'*Jaana. O meri jaana. Main hoon tere baap ka chacha ...*'

5

Mhatre always marvelled at how most portrayals of police work in films or on television in India were so completely off the mark. He himself had grown up thinking policemen's lives were all about high-speed chases, adrenaline-filled shootouts and beating up criminals in lock-ups, thanks to Bollywood.

In reality, all of this happened only once in a while. A city like Mumbai, with its horrendous traffic and bad roads, had next to nil scope for high-speed chases. Interrogations could be quite violent, but only at times. Mostly, a couple of slaps was all it took. Shootouts had ended with the encounter era. On an average, there was maybe one incident in three to four years where a policeman had to discharge his service weapon, and half of those instances were of the police firing in the air, which worked wonders. The last instance in which a policeman had shot someone dead was five years ago, and that policeman had been Mhatre himself.

Actual police investigation took a lot of legwork and was fraught with disappointments at every stage. There was also a fair amount of brainwork involved, and reliance on experience from past cases. Human behaviour was predictable. For example, the running axiom was that if there was a murder, you had to look at the immediate family first. Only those who knew the victim well enough would hate them enough to kill them.

Mhatre had started with the hotel and quickly encountered his first disappointment with the hotel's CCTV cameras. The Digital Video Recorder, which stored CCTV footage, had been burned almost to ashes. From the hotel itself, he called up the ACP in charge of the control room and requested footage from all cameras installed along the route from the CST station to the hotel. The ACP told Mhatre that he would have it sent by the end of the day. Which meant he could only see it the next day. He made a mental note to speak to Khan if the footage didn't arrive by that night. Being a DCP, Khan was senior to the Control Room ACP, and coming from him, a word would be an order, not a request.

The cause of the fire was believed to have been a short circuit, triggered due to the renovation work on the top floor, and aggravated by the presence of the flammable material. The fire brigade was conducting its own investigation into it, and would submit their report soon. Till such time as they officially called it arson, or suspected arson, there were no legal grounds to start a police investigation into that aspect.

Mhatre moved on to the next part of the investigation. The hotel employed a single cook to make tea and coffee. All other orders were outsourced to a restaurant on the same block. There were five young boys to take care of the guests' needs, apart from one very recently deceased manager.

All the five boys were at the hotel, helping Goswami, who had returned, salvage whatever they could from the burned remains. The owner sat at the reception desk on the ground floor, making an inventory of destroyed items he would have to replace. He had sacked the contractor who was renovating the place and was in talks with another one, this time for restoring the hotel to its former condition.

There were three rooms on each guest floor, making it nine rooms in all. At any given point, anything between three to seven rooms would be occupied. The fire had broken out on the third guest floor, which was being renovated. The couple in question had been staying in a room on the first floor.

Mhatre scored a mini-victory when he learned that each service boy had been assigned a floor, with the two others on standby. Which meant he only had to speak to the one boy who serviced the first floor. Time was always a precious commodity. The faster an investigation progressed, the better. Any policeman worth his salt would swear that the first forty-eight hours in any investigation were the most crucial.

He sat down on a sofa on the ground floor, which had escaped reasonably intact, with the first floor's service boy, Raman Singh, standing deferentially in front of him. The boy looked barely out of his teens.

'They didn't order anything after they checked in, saheb, but that wasn't very surprising. They checked in at around eleven in the morning but had no lunch. The fire broke out at eight in the night, too early for dinner, no? The man did most of the talking, and even that wasn't much. I only saw them once, while taking their luggage up to their room.' Raman leaned forward. 'Generous man,' he whispered. 'Tipped me a hundred rupees.'

'Good for you,' Mhatre said. 'Describe them.'

'He was wearing a pathani suit, sir. And had a full beard and a moustache. Short hair. He was going bald in places.'

'Any scars or marks?'

'Oh yes. He had a thin, vertical scar like an arc on the right cheek. Wasn't very visible, due to the beard.'

Mhatre was jotting it all down in his notepad.

'What about the woman?'

'*Uska pata nahi*, saheb.'

Mhatre looked up.

'What do you mean you don't know?'

'Arrey, she was wearing a burqa, no, saheb. How will I know what she looked like?'

Mhatre snapped his notepad shut in frustration.

'So nobody saw her face?'

'Not to my knowledge, saheb. They never stepped out of their room. And when the fire happened, we all ran for our lives.'

Mhatre nodded. It was a roadblock, but it was hardly the boy's fault.

'Do me a favour,' Mhatre said, leaning forward conspiratorially. Raman followed suit.

'Speak to the other boys. Find out if any of them saw the woman's face. Just check once. But casually. Let this be our little secret.'

Raman looked excited.

'Is she some wanted killer, saheb?'

'No, baba. *Utna bada kuch nahi hai.* But I still need to get to the bottom of this. And if you manage to give me any lead whatsoever, I'll make it worth your while.'

Raman nodded delightedly. Mhatre told him to get back to work.

It was a small trick he used frequently. Rounding up all the boys together and quizzing them would have taken longer. Plus, it would have set five tongues wagging. Journalists were already buzzing around the hotel to check if there was a juicy story to be told. Tragedy always holds potential for stories. He didn't want it known just yet that one of the guests was a person of interest to the police.

This way, Mhatre was also cultivating a potential informant for the long run. All the technology in the world aside, police investigation would never stop depending on human intelligence. If Raman was willing to gather intel for him on this case, he could be a valuable asset for other cases as well.

Mhatre stood up and went over to the owner, who was standing at the base of the staircase.

'What were the names they checked in under?' Mhatre asked him.

Goswami found the guest register among a heap of other documents on the first step of the staircase and gave him the names. Afzal and Fatima Siddiqui.

'If that woman turns up, or if anyone comes to ask about the man, let me know,' he told the owner and turned to leave.

He was almost at the door when he had a thought and turned back.

'Do you take copies of their ID proof when they check in?' he asked. As a security measure, hotel-owners had some years ago been instructed to insist on guests submitting a copy of some government-issued identification, like a passport, PAN or Aadhaar card. Most of the hotels followed the practice because it helped weed out unwanted characters and kept them out of trouble.

Goswami nodded. Together, they walked to the reception desk.

'We keep them right here,' he said, opening a drawer.

Mhatre and the owner both stared at it.

The drawer was empty.

6

Deepak Garg was pacing the living room again.

Ever since he had stopped drinking five months ago, he had been experiencing the horrible symptoms of withdrawal. He had, on many occasions, considered seeing a psychiatrist. However, he was afraid that the psychiatrist would connect his alcoholism with his wife's death and inform the police. As it is, he had only narrowly escaped being arrested for abetment to suicide, and that was only because his wife had kept his beating a secret from her parents, which was why they didn't blame him during the mandatory police PE—Preliminary Enquiry.

His son, Rohit, on the other hand, refused to even look at him, and when the police had tried to quiz him, Deepak had put his foot down, saying he did not want his distraught son to be harassed. He had no idea why his son said nothing.

Sleep had become something of a distant dream ever since he had stopped drinking. He had become so used to getting drunk to the point of passing out that his body seemed to have forgotten how to sleep on its own. There were times when he would doze off, sitting in a chair in his study, and wake up shivering and sweating. Mostly, though, he would just pace the house till early morning and manage to catch a couple of hours of sleep after dawn.

It was ironic, he thought, that the one person he had stopped drinking for—his son—had started hating him so much that they hardly ever spoke. At the beginning of every month, he would go to Rohit's room and place some money on his bed. Rohit would silently pocket it. Each month, Deepak would increase the amount slightly, as he didn't know if it was enough, and Rohit would certainly never tell him.

Their interactions had dropped to a bare minimum. At times, Deepak wanted to grab Rohit by his shoulders and shout out his apology. But he was wracked with guilt and was afraid to even touch Rohit, not knowing how the boy would react. Rohit had been a mute witness to his abusive behaviour throughout his childhood and the beginning of his teens. Deepak began to realise that forgiveness was a luxury he would never be able to hope for in this lifetime.

It was close to midnight when the latch turned and Rohit let himself in with his key. He had taken his mother's key and started using it after she died.

Rohit stepped inside, took off his shoes and saw Deepak. For a long moment, they both stared at each other.

'There's food in the kitchen,' Deepak said.

Rohit nodded.

'It's late. Is everything okay?'

Rohit nodded again.

'Anything you want to tell me?'

Rohit chuckled inwardly. As if he was going to tell this man where he had been and whom he had been with.

'No,' he said, very clearly and audibly. 'There is nothing I want to say to you.'

Deepak stared for a second, then hung his head, turned around and resumed his pacing. Rohit, too, turned around and headed to his room.

Deepak paused near the window and looked out into the night.

Help me, God, he whispered. *Help me.*

7

Mhatre had always loathed traffic. He knew that it was part of life in a city like Mumbai, but still, there was something about the whole mass of vehicles, with their horns and exhaust fumes, and the sheer clutter on the roads, that drove him crazy.

On that morning, Mhatre realised, as he navigated his bike through the rush-hour traffic on Mohammed Ali Road, that the dehydration from the previous night's drinking was making him all the more irritable.

After finishing with the hotel the previous day, he had called up JJ Hospital, where the bodies of the hotel manager and the male half of the mysterious couple, supposedly Afzal Siddiqui, were taken for post-mortem examination. The doctor conducting the autopsy, Bhupendra Trivedi, told him he would need at least one more day before he could come up with a clinical opinion. Especially, Dr Trivedi said, on Afzal Siddiqui, who was burned pretty badly. They agreed to meet the next morning.

Mhatre had returned to his office, as he had nothing else to do, and caught up on the paperwork on some of the squad's older cases. He then spent an hour touching base with his informants, and left for the bar.

Because he had reached an hour early, he ended up drinking even more than usual. He remembered talking to the manager as soon as he got there, who told him that the taxi fare from the previous night had been taken care of. Mhatre had asked about his bill from the previous night, and the manager had waved a dismissive hand.

A year ago, a customer had collapsed at the bar and died of heart failure. Even though his death was perfectly natural, or as natural as it could have been in the case of a man whose heart had given way after years of drinking and smoking, the local police station saw it as an opportunity.

For too many years, the bar had been paying the same amount of money as hafta, the fixed amount of money that has to go to the local police station in exchange for small favours like operating an hour past the given deadline and allowing smoking on the premises. A death on the premises gave the local police the chance to start a lengthy investigation, which would include uniformed policemen visiting the bar at all hours of the day or night and scaring away the clientele. The only way to stop the investigation would be an increase in the hafta.

Intersections

To the bar-owner's good fortune, however, Mhatre had taken a liking to his little establishment. Further, the death had not been the bar's fault in any manner. Its owner, after the second day of the local police station's inquiry, called up Mhatre in panic.

Mhatre took the matter up with Tamhane, who was then the DCP, Zone I. Tamhane's dislike for the police exerting their power for the sake of it and his fondness for Mhatre worked in Mhatre's and the bar-owner's favour. He called up the police station and gave the senior police inspector who was looking into the case a sharp dressing-down. From that day onwards, the bar was never bothered, and Mhatre was never given a bill at the end of his evenings there.

Mhatre knew that the bar-owner's generosity was one reason why his drinking was increasing. He also knew that the free drinks would not last forever, or that he would be expected to do something else in return soon. But at least it helped him sleep at night, without straining his finances. Alcoholism was an expensive addiction to nurture, and a policeman's salary wasn't exactly princely.

And he didn't like going home. Even to drink.

Mhatre finally entered the JJ Hospital compound and parked his bike at the first available spot he saw. Quickly, he made his way to the morgue and asked for Dr Trivedi.

The doctor was in his fifties, a man respected throughout the medical fraternity. He was something of a favourite of the police, because he loved working on medico-legal cases and went out of his way to find crucial pieces of evidence for the police wherever it was possible for him to do so.

'I always wanted to be a cop,' he told Mhatre as he led him to his office. 'But my parents would have none of it. Said it was a dirty profession and that being a doctor is more respectable.'

'You have no idea how right they were, Doctor,' Mhatre said as he settled down in the chair across the table from Trivedi.

'Don't say that,' Trivedi admonished him. 'It's your chosen profession. Respect it, no matter how it turns out.'

Mhatre felt like a chastised schoolboy. There was silence as Trivedi sat down in his chair and picked up a file from his table.

'This,' he said, sliding it across, 'is your deceased hotel guest, Afzal Siddiqui?'

Mhatre nodded. He had no reason to tell Dr Trivedi that he suspected it was an alias. In any case, he wasn't quite sure himself.

'The cause of death is pretty clear. Over 90 per cent burns. Poor man never had a chance. But you asked me about his identity. So I examined the remains pretty thoroughly.'

'And?' Mhatre asked.

'I made some interesting discoveries. Firstly, there were injuries prior to the burns.'

Intersections

Mhatre straightened up in his chair.

Trivedi hesitated before continuing.

'Bear in mind, Mr Mhatre, that this is not an exact science. We surmise what we can based on the condition of the body. The flesh, the bones, the tissue, etc.'

'I'm listening,' Mhatre said.

'So, there's an injury to his cranium. Left side, at the front. I read the panchnama. It says he was found a short distance away from the bathroom door. The panchnama also mentioned that the bathroom door has a handle made of solid metal.'

Mhatre nodded. A panchnama was a list of all the observations made at the scene of a crime or a tragedy, in the presence of five witnesses, and signed by them. Hence, *panch*-nama, a report witnessed by *five* people. One of the biggest headaches for the police was to find five people willing to sign a panchnama and then appear in court to testify whenever the case came up for hearing.

Mhatre had spoken to an officer with the MRA Marg Police Station, under whose jurisdiction the Kabootar Khana Circle fell, and asked for a copy of all the documents related to the incident. The police had filed an Accidental Death Report in the matter. As per the law, any death is either natural, homicidal or accidental. If it's homicidal, the police register a case of murder. If it falls under accidental, which can be anything from death by drowning to being run over by a car to suicide to perishing in a fire, it becomes an Accidental Death Report.

'The working theory,' Dr Trivedi disclosed, 'is that this man lost his balance, hit his head on the door handle and passed out, after which he was engulfed in the fire as it spread to the room. At some level, it makes sense. By the time the poor man woke up, he would have been on fire. The distance between the bathroom door and the spot where his body was found also supports the theory.'

'But?'

Trivedi sighed.

'I must say here that this is not something I can testify to in court,' he cautioned. 'This is a professional guess based only on experience.'

'Understood.'

Dr Trivedi paused, nevertheless, before going on.

'The burns on the man's body are extraordinarily severe, and go deep. As in, they don't seem like they were sustained after an accidental fire. They're more in sync with the body itself being set aflame.'

'I don't quite get what you're saying,' Mhatre said, although he could make a pretty good guess.

'I'm saying, I suspect there could have been two fires. The first started in the hotel — and the fire brigade will submit its own report about that. But, if I'm right, the second started in his room. When someone set his body on fire. One can always tell when a particular object, especially an object like the human body, is set on fire.'

'But you're not sure?'

'Not sure enough to testify in court, as I said. But there's another thing.'

'What?'

'The cranial injury. An experienced doctor can always tell the history of the injury based on the damage sustained by the skull.'

'What does that mean?'

'It means the injury is less consistent with him hitting his head accidentally on the door handle and more consistent with his head being hit violently by a third party.'

Mhatre took a minute to digest this.

'Dr Trivedi,' he said slowly. 'Are we looking at a murder?'

8

Mhatre lit a cigarette before making the call. Patankar answered it on the third ring.

'Bol, hero.'

'Remember the Shivaji Park incident, sir?' Mhatre asked. It was a little noisy at his end and he had to raise his voice a bit.

'Who doesn't?'

Mhatre had to smile, if joylessly. Both Patankar and Mhatre had been directly connected to the incident he was talking about.

'There was a fellow we'd picked up later. Who we thought had supplied the bomb.'

'Shekhar Bhatia,' Patankar said promptly.

'Right. Can you send me his picture?'

Patankar was curious.

'What new headache are you bringing home, Mhatre?'

'I just need to confirm something, sir. If this pans out, I'll tell you everything.'

'I can already feel my blood pressure rising,' Patankar said before hanging up.

Intersections

Quickly, he accessed the photo gallery on his computer while simultaneously marvelling how technology had changed police work. Ten years ago, he'd have had to find the right dossier from among a huge stack of files and get a photocopy of the picture, and Mhatre would have had to come down personally to collect it. Or, in an emergency, Mhatre would have had to find the nearest fax machine and Patankar would have sent the picture there.

Instead, he simply ran a search on his laptop and found the picture, which he emailed to Mhatre.

Seconds later, Mhatre threw his half-smoked cigarette on the ground, stepped on it and crossed the street to enter Sitaara Hotel. The owner was not there, but the boys were. He asked for Raman Singh and took him aside when he came down from the first floor.

'That man from the couple you took to their room?' Mhatre reminded him. 'Does this look like him?'

Mhatre showed Raman the picture of Shekhar Bhatia on his cellphone. Raman reached out hesitantly and Mhatre let him take the phone in his hand to examine the picture minutely.

Slowly, the boy nodded.

'The beard was thicker and the hair was a little different. But yes. It does look like the same man, saheb. Very much,' Raman said.

Mhatre slipped a hundred-rupee note into Raman's

shirt pocket and sent him on his way. He was aware of his heartbeat accelerating.

Before he had left JJ Hospital, Dr Trivedi had given him one last bit of information. That titbit had led to a hunch, which had now panned out.

Mhatre returned to his bike, climbed onto it but didn't start it. Instead, he lit another cigarette.

The Shivaji Park incident had been the defining moment of Mhatre's career. He was at the time a police sub-inspector posted with the Shivaji Park Police Station, fresh out of probation, young and eager and raring to go.

It was a typically pleasant Mumbai winter evening, and his assignment was to enforce security at the Shivaji Park ground, where millionaire philanthropist Chintan Mehta was going to distribute sports equipment among underprivileged children.

Mehta had burst on the city scene hardly a year ago. He would reach out to surviving victims of tragedies — floods, building collapses, road accidents, attempted murders — and not only bear all the expenses of their treatment but also provide them money till they were able to get back on their feet. The entire expense would be included in his company's Corporate Social Responsibility.

The government would announce compensation, and the bureaucrats would keep dragging their feet on the files, and all the while, Mehta slowly cemented his position in the hearts of the people.

Intersections

That day was Mehta's birthday, and he had planned to spend it doing something for the people, like he always did. The trust that ran his CSR activities had singled out fifty children from underprivileged families, who were to receive footballs, cricket bats, gloves and running shoes.

Mhatre was part of a larger detail tasked with patrolling the ground, making sure there were no such incidents as usually accompany large gatherings. The media was out in full force, as were hundreds of people who had flocked about just to get a glimpse of the man who seemed to be deeply interested in doing some good — without an agenda.

Mhatre remembered the thrill that passed through his body when he secured his service firearm in his hip holster. Although very few policemen had occasion to use it these days, the feeling of handling a weapon of death could still send a shiver down one's spine.

The man with his arm in the triangular sling caught his eye because he kept slipping his other hand under the sling. That one peculiarity led Mhatre to observe his moves more closely, and within less than a minute, he picked up several other tell-tale signs. The beads of sweat, the furtive glances and the licking of the lips.

Almost trembling, Mhatre began walking towards the man, forcing himself to stay calm, one hand firmly gripped around his wireless radio set, the other hovering over his pistol. He was halfway there when

Mehta finished distributing the sports equipment and showed signs of leaving. The media had clicked enough pictures and recorded enough videos. He had already given sound bites earlier and was now walking to his car, when a small group of people caught up to him.

'A selfie?' Mehta chuckled good-humouredly. 'With me? I'm not a film star!'

At the same time, the man with the sling started walking towards where Mehta and the group were standing. His free hand was now back under the sling. Mhatre picked up his pace, his right hand already on his gun.

Just as members of the group around Mehta raised their cellphones to click selfies, the man's hand came out from under the sling. Before Mhatre could react, the man had taken the pin out of the grenade that he was now holding in his hand.

'*Bomb!*' Mhatre shouted as he whipped out his pistol, dropped his radio and started running. Time seemed to slow down as the man, startled by Mhatre's warning, looked back once, then turned around and lobbed the grenade. His hesitation, though, had affected his aim. It went completely over Mehta's head, bounced on the roof of his car and ricocheted to the right, bang in the middle of the crowd streaming out of the ground.

The next instant, Mhatre, who was almost within touching distance of the bomber, was thrown off his feet as the grenade exploded with tremendous force. Mhatre was aware of a sharp pain in his left arm, which took the full force of his fall as he landed hard. There was a ringing in his ears that felt like it would never stop.

Even as his body reeled from the shock of the blast, his mind struggled. He forced himself to open his eyes and ignored the pain in his shoulder as he pushed himself to his feet, the shock giving way to fury.

Through the darkness engulfing his vision, he zeroed in on a single figure standing up and tearing the sling away. The bomber was just starting to run when Mhatre, who still had his pistol clutched in his right hand, raised it, grinding his teeth hard.

In a moment that would have made his shooting instructors at the Academy proud, Mhatre rested his right hand on his left palm, took aim and fired twice. The fleeing man took both hits in the back of his head, which half-disappeared in a spray of blood and brain. A girl next to him screamed as the rest of him hit the ground.

Mhatre let himself fall, and blacked out.

9

'Tujhe naa dekhun toh chain mujhe aata nahi hai, tere jitna par bhaav koi khaata nahi hai ...'

'For God's sake, sir,' Mhatre said as he walked into the squad office. 'That's one of my favourite songs!'

Patankar, who was engrossed in his cellphone, chuckled and stopped singing.

The two cops had first met two days after the Shivaji Park incident, when Mhatre was still in hospital. Patankar was with the Crime Branch at the time, in charge of its Unit V. For policing convenience, the city is divided into thirteen zones, and each has a Crime Branch unit to conduct parallel inquiries into cases registered by police stations.

Mhatre had woken up in King Edward Memorial — KEM, as it is popularly known — hospital an hour after he had blacked out, surrounded by his colleagues and seniors. His injuries were not serious. He had sustained a few stray shrapnel wounds to his face and torso, but nothing that would leave a scar.

Nobody knew of the deep and secret scarring of his mind.

The physician in charge decided to keep Mhatre under observation for a couple of days before discharging him.

That period was almost at its end when Patankar went there to visit Mhatre. Crime Branch Unit V had jurisdiction over the central Mumbai area, including Shivaji Park, and Mhatre had been expecting someone from that unit to pay him a visit eventually. Procedure demanded that an independent agency conduct a probe into incidents involving policemen discharging their firearms in the line of duty.

They had decided that Mhatre would visit the Unit V office in Kurla the next day and formally record his statement. Before leaving, Patankar had slid his chair forward and placed a hand on Mhatre's unhurt shoulder.

'In the days to come,' Patankar had said, looking deadly serious, 'a lot of people will have a lot of things to say. But hindsight is a luxury available only to those on the sidelines. What you did back there was nothing short of fucking heroic. Always remember that.'

Mhatre had felt a lump in his throat.

'Thank you, sir,' he had managed to say.

Patankar had squeezed his shoulder before standing up and walking away.

That meeting was the beginning of a professional relationship that soon turned into friendship, despite the difference in seniority and age. Mhatre was barely into the profession, while Patankar was a veteran of the encounter era, with years of experience.

'Tell me,' Patankar said, finally putting his phone away, jolting Mhatre back to the present.

'Sir, I have reason to believe that the man who burned to death at Sitaara Hotel was Shekhar Bhatia.'

Patankar straightened in his seat.

'How do you know?'

'I met Dr Trivedi at JJ Hospital this morning. Apart from an analysis of the dead man's injuries, he also told me whatever he could gather about his medical history from his remains.'

Patankar nodded. That was one reason why the police department loved Dr Trivedi. He was thorough to a fault.

'Our dead man, according to Dr Trivedi, had sustained a pretty serious fracture in his right shin, not more than three years ago.'

The expression on Patankar's face changed.

'And,' Mhatre finished, 'the boy at the hotel told me that the dead man had a scar on his right cheek. A thin, curved, vertical scar.'

'Bloody hell,' Patankar breathed. 'Bhatia's back?'

'*Was*, at least.'

The investigation into the Shivaji Park incident had been taken over by the Anti-Terrorism Squad, with the Crime Branch and the local police providing support wherever necessary. One of the tasks that was assigned to Unit V was to track down Shekhar Bhatia, an arms dealer known to provide quality arsenal to those who could afford it. It was not just this reputation that qualified Bhatia as a suspect. The investigating team had analysed the CDR of a cellphone found on the dead bomber, and had confirmed that one of the numbers frequently called from the phone was being used by Bhatia.

Patankar had called up Mhatre and asked if he was interested in being a part of the investigation team, and Mhatre did not even give it a second thought before saying yes. His reporting head, too, readily spared him and not just because Mhatre was straining at the leash. Politically, it was a good move to let a hero be involved in the investigation.

Together, Patankar and Mhatre had kicked down doors and picked up scores of suspects for questioning till they finally got a confirmed lead on Bhatia.

The two cops, thanks to an abundance of funds sanctioned by the director-general of police himself, travelled to Kolkata on the first available flight and descended on a hotel where Bhatia was supposed to be staying, with the local police providing additional manpower.

The cops got lucky. Bhatia had planned to travel to Malda and cross the border into Bangladesh. However, he had been in a road accident just a day before he fled, fracturing his right shin badly. He was sitting on the bed in his room, his leg in a plaster cast, when Patankar and Mhatre burst inside, guns raised.

After he was brought back to Mumbai, Bhatia was admitted to a hospital and kept under strict police guard for a month before the cast was removed. From there, he was handed over to the ATS and grilled for days on end, but to no avail. The evidence that the police had was less than even circumstantial. All they had was a number on a dead man's phone that an informant had said was in use by Bhatia. There was nothing conclusively linking Bhatia to the Shivaji Park incident.

Patankar and Mhatre watched with gritted teeth as Bhatia limped out of the ATS headquarters with his lawyer. He seemed to have disappeared thereafter.

Till now, if Dr Trivedi was to be believed.

'If Bhatia risked coming back to Mumbai, it had to have been for a pretty good reason,' Mhatre said.

'But that also solves at least one mystery,' Patankar said. 'Whatever reason prompted him to come here couldn't have been legal. Which is why the woman with him never turned up again. She would have had to face a lot of uncomfortable questions.'

'Which also means finding her is a priority,' Mhatre said.

Patankar sighed.

'How sure are we that he was killed?' he asked. 'Because if he was, that woman becomes our strongest suspect. She had the opportunity, for sure. But what was the motive?'

'Only she can answer that,' Mhatre replied.

Both cops sat silently for a minute, trying to figure out what their next step should be.

'I'll talk to Khan sir tomorrow,' Patankar said finally. 'Not sure how interested he'll be, especially when the possibility of murder is so flimsy at this stage.'

'Still,' Mhatre insisted. 'The very fact that Bhatia came back to Mumbai after five years needs to be investigated.'

'It's not me that you need to convince, Bajirao Singham,' Patankar said.

Mhatre chuckled at the snide comparison to the dogged, goodie-goodie policeman in the eponymous blockbuster, and nodded. It was already evening. After the kind of day he'd had, he deserved a drink.

He stood up and turned to leave.

'Uday,' Patankar said, and Mhatre turned back.

'You still think about them?' Patankar asked.

The inquiry by Unit V had been short. Fortunately, Mhatre had not lost his firearm when he blacked out at Shivaji Park. If he had, it would have brought on a bureaucratic nightmare. But the first policeman who ran to help Mhatre that evening had had the good sense to pick up his gun before it fell into civilian hands.

Mhatre had recorded his statement, recounting every detail possible, and the Crime Branch had submitted a report stating that Mhatre acted like any other policeman would have in the situation. Certain human rights groups tried to make some noise about recklessly firing a gun in the middle of a crowd, but the police commissioner himself issued a stern statement, cutting them down.

'The man lobbed a grenade at civilians. Five people died. No one had any idea what else he could have been armed with, or what his further intentions could have been. PSI Uday Mhatre, despite being the juniormost officer on the scene, displayed exemplary presence of mind and dedication to duty, without paying heed to his own injuries,' the commissioner had said.

Five people died.

The commissioner had said it matter-of-factly. Which was easy for him.

Mhatre had read the report after being discharged from the hospital. As per procedure, the First Information Report was registered at the Shivaji Park Police Station before being taken over by the ATS.

Shireen Bhat, nineteen years old. She was from Kashmir and was visiting the city with her father when she heard of Mehta's charity event and decided to attend it.

Reema Malhotra, twenty-six years old. A sales executive who worked five minutes away from

Intersections

Shivaji Park. Her son was only a year old when she was killed.

Sehar Siddiqui, five years old. Her parents had brought her to see the man whose donations allowed them to put their life back together after their old house collapsed four years ago. She had managed to wriggle her hand free from her mother's and run a short distance ahead when the grenade exploded.

Head Constable Vasant Patil, forty-two years old. He was posted with the traffic police and was regulating the vehicular flow outside the ground.

Ashok Singh, twenty-two years old. He had had to give up his dream of becoming a footballer because his financial condition didn't allow it. But he wanted his younger brother to pursue the same dream and had hence come to collect a football from Mehta.

'You do, don't you?' Patankar persisted, looking intently at Mhatre.

'Some things you manage to forget, sir,' Mhatre replied tonelessly. 'Some things burn a hole into your heart and make a home in it.'

Patankar didn't know what to say.

'I'll see you tomorrow, sir,' Mhatre said and walked out of the office.

10

The first night after being discharged from the hospital had been the worst.

He kept seeing blood on his hands every time he looked at them. The entire night, he lay tossing and turning on his bed, unable to get the faces out of his mind.

Closing his eyes was worse. Not only did he see visions of faces melting into blood and tissue, he heard voices calling his name. Calling him names. Bad names.

Halfway into the night he got off his bed and started pacing. When that didn't work, he stripped off his shirt and began working out, although his body felt sore. He started with stretching exercises and moved on to push-ups, making his muscles tense and ache. It was only after he completed four sets of twenty-five push-ups each – and felt no different after it all – that he realised it was going to be of no use.

He then spent what seemed like an eternity sitting motionlessly on the bed, letting his body calm down and the sweat dry off. Then he stood up, got dressed and walked out of his house.

He had no idea how long he had walked till he came to the all-night bar. The neon lights over the entrance seemed to reflect the faces he did not want to see. Quickly, he ducked into the semi-darkness inside and sat at a table.

As the liquor made its way down his throat and mixed with his bloodstream, the storm in his mind seemed to start settling down. After the first quarter of rum, he tried closing his eyes. The bloody faces were still there.

He ordered another quarter. It became a game, closing his eyes at frequent intervals as the liquor continued to dull his senses. At least he wasn't seeing blood on his hands anymore. At least there were no voices now.

Three quarters later, he finally accepted that the faces were always going to be there. But he also realised that the liquor gave him the courage to look at them.

He went home late the next morning in a taxi called by the bar manager, too drunk to walk, barely able to tell the driver his address. That was the first time it happened, and it wouldn't be the last.

The sudden buzzing of his cellphone shook Mhatre out of his memories. Absently, he reached out and grabbed the phone, squinting at the morning light streaming in through his window.

'Come early. Might have a problem,' the text message from Patankar said.

Mhatre frowned and tried to rack his brains to remember what he had done in the recent past that

Patankar would regard as a problem. His superior officer for the most part oscillated between supportiveness and tolerance towards Mhatre's methods.

'What happened?' he texted.

The reply came within seconds.

'Bhai, tu aa jaldi.'

Mhatre shrugged and hurriedly bathed and dressed.

Patankar's answer suggested something that occurred to him while he was picking up his bike from outside the bar an hour-and-a-half later. He wasn't really sure, but it was the strongest possibility.

Sitting astride his bike, he made a call and spoke for a couple of minutes before hanging up and putting on his helmet. His suspicion was now all but confirmed.

As he pulled up at the Colaba Police Station, Patankar was waiting by the squad office, leaning against one of the two police SUVs assigned to the squad.

'Khan called,' he said.

'Let me guess,' Mhatre replied. 'Those three we'd detained. The ones we released the day the Sitaara Hotel fire broke out.

'How the hell did you know?' Patankar asked, tossing him the keys to the SUV. 'Let's talk on the way,' he said. 'Khan wants to see us.'

Mhatre first took a long drink of water from the bottle placed in the holder between the two front seats. Then he checked his face in the mirror. His eyes were a little bloodshot, but there was nothing he could do about that.

Turning the key, he started the ignition and pulled out of the compound.

A day before the Sitaara Hotel fire, Mhatre had picked up three history-sheeters. Niyaz Ansari, Tahir Siddiqui and Usman Ahmed. All three of them had lengthy and serious records of crimes, including armed robbery, kidnapping with robbery and robbery with assault. They weren't strictly a gang as such, but were known to work together when the occasion demanded.

It was a routine tip-off from an informant Mhatre had cultivated way back when he was at the Shivaji Park Police Station. The informant had called him saying he had seen all three of them together near Plaza Cinema. Mhatre had sped to the spot with five constables and had intercepted them just as they were on their way out of a restaurant.

As it turned out, none of them had a firearm or anything else that might indicate that they were planning a crime. Nevertheless, the very fact that they were together was enough grounds, prima facie, for a routine detention. They were all bundled into the vehicle and taken to the squad office.

Mhatre and Patankar took turns grilling them for hours but to no avail, which was hardly surprising as all three were hardened criminals with several stays in central jails behind them. They were held overnight and till the next evening, when the stipulated twenty-four-hour period was due to run out.

'Apparently, Tahir Siddiqui has submitted a complaint to Khan,' Patankar said.

'What the fuck!' Mhatre snapped. Patankar was the only superior he could speak to like that in private.

'Claims you assaulted him in the lock-up and held him beyond the legal time limit,' Patankar said.

Mhatre shook his head.

'Is that the best that Soman could come up with?'

'What was that?' Patankar asked, looking interested.

Dhananjay Soman was the senior police inspector in charge of the Colaba Police Station. Since the squad didn't have a lock-up of their own, their suspects were held in the Colaba lock-up. Soman, a thoroughly insecure and only occasionally successful cop, who did not appreciate an independent squad reporting directly to his DCP in his own compound, had taken it upon himself to make things difficult for them.

'I spoke to someone in Colaba on my way. Soman was seen talking to our three heroes when we put them in the lock-up for the night.'

'*Gandu...*' Patankar said under his breath.

Minutes later, Mhatre and Patankar were sitting in front of Khan.

Intersections

'You were supposed to submit a report about this to me, Mhatre,' Khan said.

'I'm sorry, sir. The fire broke out immediately after our conversation and things got busy after that. Especially in the light of suspicions about that woman we've been hunting.'

'Have you found her?' Khan snapped.

'No, sir.'

'And you still haven't found time to write up a simple report about what you claim was a routine detention?'

'It was, sir.'

Khan leaned back in his seat.

'What do you think it is we do here, Mhatre?' he asked. 'This posting, this independent squad, do you think it absolves you of the boring aspects of the job, like paperwork? You think you're above all of that.'

'That's not true, sir,' Mhatre said, taking care to keep his eyes lowered.

'Isn't it?' Khan roared. 'Let me point out: had you submitted that report to me the next morning like I'd asked you to, I would have had your version of the events, duly dated and signed, *before* this bloody complaint landed on my desk. Now, even if you do submit it to me in the next one minute, it is still going to be viewed as damage control. And don't you dare suggest pre-dating your report. I'm not going to lie on your behalf if this shit leads to a serious inquiry!'

Mhatre said nothing.

'If I may, sir ...' Patankar cut in carefully.

'What?' Khan snapped, swivelling towards the older cop.

'If I may talk to you for a minute, sir ...?'

Khan took a second to understand.

'Oh, sure. I need to talk to you too.'

'Uday,' Patankar said, looking meaningfully at his junior. Mhatre caught his look, then nodded and stood up. He brought his fists to the seams of his jeans, raised his heels once, brought them down smartly, turned around and walked out.

Outwardly, he appeared calm. Inwardly, he was seething as he got into the parked vehicle and took his cellphone out. He lit a cigarette, not really caring if someone saw him smoking, and went through the pictures one by one—again.

Shireen. Reema. Sehar. Vasan—

Mhatre froze.

No, he thought. *No, that can't be right.*

Quickly, he closed the photo gallery and looked for the number he needed to call.

11

'Sir, I understand how this looks, but the petty politics behind this complaint also needs to be taken into account,' began Patankar.

'Can we prove it?' Khan asked. 'I know and you know that Soman is capable of these things. But is there any evidence?'

Patankar said nothing.

'Look,' Khan said. 'The complaint is a flimsy one and might not lead to anything. But I need to sanction at least a preliminary enquiry just to cover our bases. There needs to be a record of the fact that we received a complaint and took some action on it. In the meantime, please tell Mhatre to stay away from all three of them. The last thing we need is for him to make matters worse.'

'Yes, sir.'

'What's the progress on that woman from Sitaara Hotel?'

Patankar succinctly brought Khan up to speed on the investigation so far.

'And you're sure this man who died in the fire was Shekhar Bhatia?' Khan asked, peering at him closely. He had clearly not expected the investigation to take this turn.

'We only have the hotel attendant's version and our own photographs of Bhatia to go on right now, sir. But as the two people who hunted and interrogated Bhatia back then, both Uday and I are reasonably sure.'

'Stay on it. See where it leads. But keep it quiet. I don't want the press crowding around asking questions until I have some answers.'

'Right, sir.'

'Where are you on CCTV footage?'

'The control room hasn't yet sent the footage from around the hotel that we requested, sir. We were going to follow up this morning, but ...' Patankar shrugged.

'I'll talk to them.'

Patankar stood up to leave, but Khan intercepted him with another question, one he'd wanted to ask him from the beginning.

'What's the deal with Mhatre, Patankar?'

Patankar turned around curiously.

'I mean,' Khan explained, 'one minute he's showing some really good initiative and spotting an anomaly which everyone else seems to have missed. The next minute, I have a complaint against him on my desk. And I'm hearing reports about him drinking heavily every night. What's going on with him? Did that incident at Shivaji Park really affect him that much?'

Patankar took a minute before answering.

'That incident ... well, I was involved, too, and I saw him up close. He'd spend hours going over the file and reading about those five people who died, again and again.'

'But that wasn't his fault!'

'That was never under doubt, sir. But having five innocent people die on your watch for no fault of theirs, five families broken forever, and to witness that happen so early in your career ... one can never tell how someone might react to senseless tragedy.'

Khan had to agree. He had seen the same too many times in his career.

'I think,' Patankar went on, 'everything Uday has done since then is to prevent another five people from dying on his watch. I don't think he'll be able to take it if another attack like that takes place, and he discovers he could have prevented it in any way, big or small.'

There was silence before Khan spoke again.

'The boy is veering too close to the edge.'

'Unfortunately, that's what it seems like, sir.'

'Which means we have to watch over him. Which is also why I am necessary in this whole equation. I am not questioning your efficiency as a senior officer, but you're too personally involved. Both with him and the incident. If you're the proverbial good cop here, I have to be the bad cop, whether he likes it or not.'

This time, too, Patankar said nothing.

'Especially now that he believes Shekhar Bhatia came back to the city.'

'If he did, sir, and it does seem like he did, it can't have been for any good reason,' Patankar reasoned.

'I get that. So carry on. Let me know what you find. But till this matter of the complaint blows over, stay watchful.'

Patankar nodded, clicked his heels and left. He made his way down the staircase to the compound where the SUV was parked. Mhatre was sitting on the hood talking on his phone.

'Okay … okay … thanks a lot. I'll see you soon.'

Mhatre ended the call.

'No,' Patankar said, as Mhatre turned to him.

'What?'

'That look. I know that look. And before you say anything, the answer is no.'

Mhatre fished his packet of cigarettes out of his pocket. Patankar glanced down and saw two cigarette butts on the ground.

'Tahir Siddiqui,' Mhatre said, taking out another cigarette from the pack.

'What about him?'

'He was the weakest link in the chain. He has the least serious record and had he not been hanging out with Niyaz Ansari and Usman Ahmed, we wouldn't even have picked him up. Do you agree, sir?'

Patankar nodded reluctantly. Siddiqui was small fry who got his kicks from associating with the more hard-core criminals.

'So how did he suddenly grow the balls to file a complaint against cops?'

Patankar's face changed. Mhatre could see the gears grinding in his head.

'That did occur to me when I first heard about it this morning. But there was too much else going on …'

'Let's think about it now. He's made a living from assisting the likes of Ansari and Ahmed in small capacities on their jobs. I just checked his record with the Modus Operandi Bureau. The most serious charge he has against him is attempted armed robbery, and the weapon was a chopper. And now he's taking on the Mumbai Police? And I don't mean to sound egoistic on behalf of the force here but …'

'I know what you mean!' Patankar said impatiently.

'Who benefits?' Mhatre went on. 'This inquiry, even if there is a proper inquiry, will blow over within days. He has no evidence. We didn't even rough him up—that much. Medical tests will show no assault. Soman, for all his scheming, is hardly going to record a statement in Tahir Siddiqui's favour.'

All allegations of assault, custodial or otherwise, required the complainant to get a medical certificate detailing their injuries, which became part of the evidence. The police, of course, had, over the years, figured out parts of the human anatomy that did not hold bruises or marks for long. Plus, like Mhatre said, Siddiqui wasn't even hit beyond a couple of whacks to the head. The focus had been on Ansari and Ahmed.

'The other two,' Patankar said. 'They benefit. Siddiqui submits a complaint and the other two automatically become off limits for us till the matter has blown over. It was these two who actually prodded him to submit that complaint.'

'Maybe Soman did plant the seed in their head, after which they hit upon this idea. And they surely lost no time. Why? What do they have to hide, for them to go to these lengths to prevent us from picking them up again in the near future?'

It took a few seconds for Patankar to see Mhatre's point. Mhatre took the time to light another cigarette.

'*Arrey, bhenchod* ...' Patankar said finally.

Mhatre nodded vigorously.

When they were working together on the Shivaji Park incident, they had picked up a lot of history-sheeters known to be associated with Bhatia in their hunt for the arms supplier. It was through this patient and dogged questioning of scores of suspects that they'd finally got a lead on Bhatia's location.

One of them was Niyaz Ansari.

Now Bhatia had fetched up dead in a hotel in south Mumbai. And Ansari was doing everything he could to avoid being grilled by the police.

Intersections

Both Patankar and Mhatre had the same thought as they looked at each other. They didn't have to say it out loud.

The bastard knows something.

12

'Ms Rupa!'

Rupa stopped and turned around. It took her a moment to locate the short, portly Ms Kritika, who was hurrying towards her, a thick pile of books tucked under one arm.

'Let me take those,' Rupa said as Ms Kritika caught up with her. She gently but firmly took the books, and they resumed walking towards the staff room together.

From his spot in the corner of the college campus, Rohit watched silently. It seemed to him that Rupa looked more beautiful with each passing day.

When they started their romance, they had established one ground rule: in college they would behave like teacher and student. Rohit was sure that, one day, no matter when the day came, she would be equally willing to come out in the open. But he understood her apprehensions and was willing to give her as long as she needed.

What's a few years when this is going to last a lifetime, he told himself every time he felt himself growing impatient.

Looking at his wristwatch, he realised it was almost time for his lecture to begin. He couldn't care less for physics and he hated the lecturer. But it was only because of Rupa that he was making the effort to learn.

The sound levels in the classroom seemed to drop by a notch as he walked in, his head down, one hand holding the strap of his bag, the other in his pocket. He was the symbol of tragedy in his class. The boy who'd lost his mother. Boys and girls he never knew existed would shoot him looks of sympathy.

At least his mother's tragic death had changed their attitude towards him. Earlier, he would be at the receiving end of all the bullying. The atmosphere at home had affected his behaviour and he seldom mixed with his classmates, choosing to be alone and speaking only when spoken to. For teenagers, he was the perfect target for cruel practical jokes.

That stopped when his mother died. Out of basic human decency — or sheer pity — they stopped picking on him. He was only too happy to be finally left alone.

Only Rupa understood him. She had once seen him sitting in a classroom, reading a book — this was before the 'accident' that took his mother from him — while everyone else was in the grounds. She asked him why he wasn't outside with the others, and he told her he would get roughed up the minute he set foot on the grounds.

'Don't fear them,' she told him. 'Pity them. They are only reacting to what they don't understand. You're different from them. It doesn't make you wrong—or their behaviour right.'

And so, he fell in love.

When his mother died, Rupa sought him out after classes and drew him aside.

'If you ever want to talk,' she told him, 'don't hesitate to come to me.'

He just nodded his thanks and turned away, to hide the worship in his eyes. As he approached the campus gate, however, he stopped. He stood for a long moment, thinking hard, and then turned around and walked to the staff room. He caught up with her just as she was about to enter.

'Do you like beaches?' he asked.

She looked puzzled but nodded.

'I stay close to Girgaum Chowpatty. I am mostly there in the evenings.'

She offered a little smile.

'I'll see you there one of these days,' she said.

He smiled too.

That evening, he paced the length of the beach till he saw her coming. He almost ran up to her.

'You came,' was all he could say.

'I stay close by. And I like this beach too,' she said.

Intersections

They sat down at the far end of the beach and talked for hours. He did most of the talking, while she was content listening to him.

Over the next two months, they shared almost every evening together at the beach. Slowly, all the anguish that had built up over the years started pouring out.

'You should tell the police,' she said the night he talked about his mother's death.

He shook his head.

'I can't do that to my grandparents. Right now, they are at least living under the illusion that their daughter had a happy marriage.'

She looked at him tenderly before reaching out and taking his hand. It was the first time she did that.

'You're an incredibly strong person,' she said softly.

Without warning, he burst into tears. She moved close to him and pulled him into an embrace, and held him long after he stopped crying.

'Rohit!'

Mr Sadanand's stern voice jolted him out of his thoughts.

'Your assignment, please.'

He nodded and picked up the printout on his desk.

'Right here, sir,' he said, standing up and walking up to the physics teacher. He had promised himself he would do better in studies. Because it would make *her* happy.

13

Every police unit, station, crime branch and special squad has its own in-house expert on technical investigation. It can be an officer or a constable, but the basic framework of this cop is the same. They take a liking to the technical aspects of an investigation early on in their career and over the years start expanding their knowledge, reading up on the latest methods of detection, reports and studies till they become their unit's go-to person for all things technical.

In the Zone I squad, this expert was API Sushmita Kadam.

In a male-dominated force, and even more male-dominated bastion of technical experts, Kadam was an exception. The thirty-year-old strikingly pretty cop had been studying software engineering when she cracked the MPSC exams on her second attempt and got selected as a police sub-inspector.

While she was equally efficient at other aspects of policing, analysis of CDRs and CCTV camera footage was Kadam's forte. It was not an unfamiliar sight to see her tapping away at her laptop, seated ramrod straight in her chair in one corner of the squad office till late hours of the night, tracking some fresh lead in an ongoing investigation or culling out corroborative evidence for old cases that were soon to go to trial.

Even if Niyaz Ansari was physically off-limits for the Zone I squad, his movements were not. Mhatre had called up Kadam from outside Khan's office and told her what he needed. He also gave her Ansari's current number, which he had noted down when he seized his phone after detaining him. Kadam listened patiently, responded crisply and got down to work.

By the time Patankar and Mhatre got back to the office, Kadam had CDRs of Ansari's number for the last two months in her email inbox. Every police force sets up a comfortable working relationship with cellular service-providers that ensures CDRs are sent as soon as they are requested for. In most of the cases that land on a policeman's desk, a CDR might hold a crucial clue about the movement or whereabouts of a wanted accused that might lead to speedy arrest.

Kadam nodded to Patankar and Mhatre as they passed by, Patankar singing, '*Mausam mastaana, paise nastaana, ekach quarter tighaat pyavi lagel bastaana.*'

Kadam stuck a lozenge in her mouth and sat back in her chair, two separate stacks of paper in her hand. For the average cop, CDR analysis can be tedious and boring. For those who like it, however, it can be fun.

The first stack was all the calls made and received by Ansari over the last two months. The primary objective here was to establish if Ansari had been in direct touch with Bhatia before his death. If the CDRs established that, it would give the squad definite grounds to pick him up for questioning; even Khan could not deny them permission to do so, inquiry or no inquiry. The two-month margin would make the job lengthier, but was necessary. Better safe than sorry was such a fundamental rule of crime investigation that the adage might as well have been coined with the profession in mind.

The other stack was a record of his cellular movements. In this respect, Kadam shared Mhatre's contempt for movies and television shows, and their portrayal of crime detection techniques. Cellular location mapping was never an exact science, at least not in India. It only showed the location of the cellular tower through which the subject's phone had passed at any given time, and that was a wide radius, leaving the rest of the job to deduction and legwork.

Kadam started with the call records. She accessed the database on her laptop which held details of all history-sheeters known to the squad so far. As the in-house geek, she was the de facto keeper of this database anyway.

One by one, she started typing out the numbers that Ansari had called, or had received calls from, over the last one week, in the search bar to check for any matches. This was as much for elimination as for clues. Given his background, the fact that Ansari would fraternise with other history-sheeters was no surprise. But if any particular name occurred too often, or seemed out of place, that name became a lead.

Kadam searched for those numbers that did not throw up a hit on Truecaller. The app had become something of a boon for a lot of professions when it came to identifying owners of cellphone numbers, and the police were no exception.

Kadam was almost at the end of her list when she came across a number that made her pause. It was a Gujarat number that did not have any details either in her database or on Truecaller. In a time when almost everyone had their numbers updated on Truecaller, either by themselves or someone else, this was a rarity. In the eyes of an investigator, who is trained to look at everything with suspicion, it also suggested that its owner preferred to stay unidentified to the world at large.

She picked up the entire stack of call records and started looking for the number. By the time she finished, she was smiling.

The next thing she did was to open her email and send out a fresh request, this time for the CDRs of this number. Till the service-provider reverted, there was nothing to do on that front.

Then she picked up Ansari's CDRs and walked to Patankar's cabin. He and Mhatre were having a smoke when she got to the door.

'Turn the fan on, please,' she said, startling both of them. Patankar immediately flicked on a switch, mumbling an apology. Both of them stubbed out their cigarettes.

'You have something already?' Mhatre asked with mild awe.

'I might,' she said enigmatically, sitting down on the chair next to him. 'This is a number that Ansari has been in contact with for the last two weeks. It caught my attention because there's nothing on it on Truecaller. At this point, it's just a hunch.'

'But?' Patankar asked.

'Purely drawing from experience, I think it is a new SIM card, bought recently and used for specific purposes and a limited period of time. What Hollywood calls a "burner phone". Used for the duration of the job and then disposed of.'

The two men nodded.

'It first made contact with Ansari fourteen days ago, and they have exchanged calls seven more times after that. I'm still waiting for this number's CDRs.'

'What was the last call? Incoming or outgoing? And when?'

'Outgoing. Ansari called this number and spoke for a brief sixteen seconds. That was four days ago.'

Intersections

Mhatre and Patankar looked at each other.

'Yes,' Kadam said, interpreting their look. 'The day of the Sitaara Hotel fire. Ansari must have called it immediately after being released from here, while you …' she turned to Mhatre, '… were in Khan sir's office.'

'Call it,' Patankar said, opening a drawer in his desk and taking out a cellphone. It was a trick he had learned from his days in the Crime Branch. Always keep a couple of spare cellphones handy, to be used for such occasions. Cellphones with numbers that had no details on Truecaller to identify who was calling.

Kadam took the phone from Patankar and dialled the number.

'It's ringing,' she said.

She let it ring out before disconnecting the call and trying again. The call connected once again and Kadam waited. She was just about to hang up when it was answered. She swiftly activated the speaker mode.

'Good afternoon, sir, this is Arpika from your bank,' Kadam said, putting on her cheeriest 'customer service' voice. 'We have a couple of new loan offers I thought I'd discuss with you. Is now a good time?'

There was a pause. Then a gruff voice spoke at the other end.

'Do you know the owner of this phone?'

All three cops looked at each other, confused.

'I … I don't understand … who is this?' Kadam asked.

'This is Senior Police Inspector Vishwas Kamble, MRA Marg Police Station. The owner of this phone passed away in a fire in our jurisdiction four days ago. We're trying to trace his family, and any help you can give us will be appreciated.'

14

The first night was the worst.

She kept seeing blood on her hands, even though it had been washed away hours ago, and was afraid to look at a mirror lest she see blood on her face as well. Closing her eyes only made her see the same scene again ... and again. Every time she saw it, she felt as if something warm and sticky was being thrown at her.

Getting down on her knees, she turned to the only solace that she knew. She clasped her hands together to pray, but stopped. She was scared to close her eyes.

Taking deep breaths and summoning all the courage that she had, she lowered her eyelids, the prayer ready on her lips. But as soon as her eyes shut, she saw a flash of red and felt the warm stickiness crawl over her again. Stifling a scream, she stood and ran out into the darkness.

She jumped over the wall of the compound the way she had so many times in the past, when she was a carefree young girl escaping from a world of rules for a few hours with her friends. Only this time, she was trying to escape something else entirely.

She walked on briskly as the city buzzed around her with the form of energy that only comes at night. She walked, her arms around herself, past indifferent neon lights, curious street urchins and lustful predators prowling the streets. She walked, through whistles, catcalls, car horns and other sounds that seemed to bounce off her, never really reaching her ears.

When the hand clamped itself in a vice-like grip over her mouth and dragged her into the alley, she didn't even realise it till the other hand reached down and slid up her skirt. She started struggling as she was pushed roughly against a wall, the hard body with its male smell pressing against her. She shut her eyes in pain as the hand pressed over her mouth more tightly, and once again felt the horror washing over her. She opened her eyes wide and the first thing she saw was a bottle of beer, with a smashed serrated edge, jutting out of a garbage can in the alley.

Wordlessly, she reached out, gripped it and traced a slow, deliberate carving path into the body pressed against her. The broken edge of the bottle sliced, quick and clean, through the man's belly. As his grip loosened, she drove the bottle through his throat, cutting off his scream before it could come out.

As his blood spurted forward, she closed her eyes. Having gone through the same feeling only hours ago, she didn't even flinch as she was bathed in the man's blood.

As always, she woke up sweating, her heart beating hard, as the blood spurted out of the man's throat.

Intersections

Getting off the bed, she went to the bathroom and splashed cold water over her face several times. Then she stood hunched over the wash basin, the water dripping from her face. She looked at the mirror above, into her own eyes. And she liked what she saw. They were no longer the eyes of a scared teenager.

She dried her face and came out of the bathroom just as her cellphone started buzzing. The number was not one known to her, but she never stored numbers in her phone anyway. There was only one person with whom she had maintained steady contact throughout her life, and she had that number committed to memory. The rest of them were just visitors to her life. She neither anticipated nor cared for any kind of permanent relationship with any of them.

She answered the call and put the phone to her ear, saying nothing.

'It's me,' Niyaz Ansari said, after a couple of seconds. He found the woman unnerving and had only agreed to work with her because Bhatia had vouched for her.

'Hmm,' was all she offered by way of response.

'I've taken care of the cops. I don't think they'll be bothering me anytime soon.'

'Are you using the same cellphone you were using earlier?' she asked.

There was a pause.

'Ye-yes ... Why?'

'Because I'm pretty sure the cops have this number now. Get a new SIM card and handset. And get new ones for me as well.'

'Handset too?' Ansari asked.

'Those can be tracked by themselves, you know,' she reminded him, a touch of condescension creeping into her voice.

'Ummm ... right. Sorry,' Ansari said. The woman was already making him nervous, and he didn't like it.

'What else?' she asked.

'You said you wanted to meet?'

'Bandstand. Tomorrow evening. Be there by six-thirty,' she said, and hung up abruptly.

They called her 'Chhaaya'. Shadow. And that was a reputation she had cultivated with great effort and care. She was not going to let a small-time hoodlum ruin it because he couldn't use his head.

From her call records, she jotted down Ansari's number on the back of an ATM receipt in case she needed to contact him before he met her the next day. That was the only reason she preserved ATM receipts. Then she removed the SIM card from her handset and returned to the bathroom, where she flushed it down the toilet.

Then, she took the handset and threw it on the floor with all the force she could muster, which was considerable. She picked it up and repeated the action, and this time, it came apart in several pieces.

She collected them and tossed them in a bag that she would discard later in a public trashcan.

Next, she walked to the phone on the table.

'Yes, it's me from Room 302. I'm afraid I'll have to check out in an hour. No, no, nothing like that. Just a personal emergency.'

15

Someone, Mhatre didn't remember who, had once described crime investigation and detection as a cat-and-mouse game between the suspect and the investigator. It was hardly an original description and among the most clichéd ones. Mhatre didn't care much for clichés. But he also had to appreciate that the comparison was an apt one.

As he lit a cigarette, Mhatre also had to marvel at the sheer multitude of ways in which one could circumvent direct orders if one put their mind to it. Tracking Ansari's CDRs was just one thing that Mhatre had put into motion.

Because criminals always have outnumbered policemen, and always will, police forces, over the years, have established their own ways to deal with the problem. An official method was to set up Mohalla Committees—citizens' groups in the jurisdiction of each police station to ensure law and order. Another was the Police Mitra scheme, where civilians were recruited to be the eyes and ears of the police force. No

Intersections

Police Mitra, however, was really going to risk his life ratting on a hard-core criminal. The system worked well when pursuing petty criminals, but not when it came to the more dangerous ones.

This is where the khabri network came in. The informants were known by a variety of descriptive names. Mhatre's favourite was 'tipper', slang for one who provides a tip-off.

All cops worthy of their jobs start cultivating informants from the very beginning of their career. Some of them, if they prove themselves to be trustworthy, turn into much more than mere tip-givers. They begin to do more than just tip off their patron cops, including the not-so-innocuous jobs of fuelling their vices. They stop being known as tippers and are then given the title of *khaas aadmi*.

Mhatre's khaas aadmi was named Baban Sahu. A migrant from Jharkhand with no fixed job, Sahu had drifted through numerous low-paying jobs all over the city and hence had friends everywhere. He also had a nose for gossip and a completely nondescript appearance, which made him the ideal candidate to be assigned to shadow someone.

Sahu's assignment today was Niyaz Ansari. His current job was to sell ice cream on a bicycle, and the mobility allowed him to go just about anywhere in the city. The business had been set up with Mhatre's help, so Sahu did not report to anyone, nor was he limited to a particular area.

Early that morning, a day after the Zone I Squad discovered what they regarded as a definite link between Ansari and Bhatia, Sahu set up his bicycle across the street from Ansari's house in Madanpura. Next to him was his friend's motorbike. Sahu had arrived at an agreement with this friend who stayed in the same area; he had agreed to loan him his motorbike and pick up his bicycle when required.

Sahu spent the entire day selling ice cream, slipping hundred-rupee notes to two local cops who tried to drive him away, and even made a decent profit in the process. Mhatre's orders were clear: Sahu was not to invoke his name unless it was an emergency. A beat constable looking for a bribe under the guise of driving away unauthorised hawkers hardly qualified as an emergency. In Mumbai, it was life as usual.

Sahu waited with patience, which he was blessed with abundantly, till Ansari left his house on his motorbike at around five in the evening. Sahu made a quick call to Mhatre and his friend, and set off in covert pursuit.

He trailed Ansari all the way to Churchgate Railway Station, where he parked his bike near Ansari's in the pay-and-park lot, and boarded the same train that Ansari did, taking care to keep his distance. He encountered his first problem at Bandra Railway Station, where Ansari got off the train. He had no easy way of knowing where Ansari was to go from there and didn't have a vehicle to trail whatever mode of public transport Ansari took. Getting into the first available auto rickshaw and saying 'follow that man' only worked in the movies. It never worked in real life, simply because no auto rickshaw driver wanted to get embroiled in anything that spelled trouble.

Fortunately, Sahu was able to think on his feet. Ansari headed for the spot where auto rickshaws dropped off their fares outside the station and Sahu got close to his target. It was evening and the place was crowded, which made it easier. As Ansari struggled to find an auto rickshaw, Sahu was right behind him, pretending to try to catch the same auto rickshaw. As a result, he heard Ansari loud and clear when he told the auto driver his destination. The auto driver refused, but Sahu had the information he needed.

Quickly, Sahu broke away and went to another spot around fifty metres away, where, he knew from experience, he could get an auto rickshaw quicker. He got one on the second attempt.

'Bandstand,' he told the driver. 'As fast as you can, please.'

By the time Ansari got off at the promenade, having finally got an auto after ten minutes of trying, Sahu was waiting for him and saw him alight. He had already texted Mhatre about the destination.

He saw Ansari go up to and sit down next to a woman wearing a burqa. She slid close to him as soon as he sat down, and took his hand.

'Sir, *lagta he woh apni gf se milra he,*' Sahu texted Mhatre from his post, partly hidden behind a tree.

It took Mhatre a second to decode the text message. He knew 'gf' stood for 'girlfriend' and 'milra he', he realised, was Sahu's version of *'mil raha hai'*.

He felt a little twinge of doubt. Was Ansari really just spending time with his girlfriend at a popular destination for couples? It was not unheard-of for gangsters to find romantic partners, and despite all his convictions about Ansari, he was apprehensive about making the wrong assumption, especially if acting on it meant going against Khan's orders.

'Ruk ja udhar. Nazar rakh,' he texted Sahu back, thinking hard. He was in his office, and logically he had no reason to be in Bandra during working hours. Which meant he had to circumvent the system yet again.

Opening his contacts list in his cellphone, he found the number he was looking for and called it. The call was answered on the fourth ring.

'Am I speaking to the handsomest cop in the Mumbai Crime Branch?' Mhatre asked.

'No, but I'm speaking to the best liar in Zone I,' API Devendra Sathe replied dryly.

Sathe was posted with the Crime Branch Unit IX, which took care of the Bandra–Andheri belt. He was also a batchmate of Mhatre's, and the bond that is forged during the training period seldom breaks, be it among the junior officers or the IPS cadre. The best person you can ask a favour from is your batchmate. It's an unwritten rule in the police force. Your batchmate always has your back.

In a few words, Mhatre told Sathe what he wanted from him. Sathe was reluctant to comply, but he was also perceptive enough to realise that Mhatre really needed something.

'Okay, but I'm doing this without telling any of my seniors, so you owe me,' Sathe said.

'That's a promise, brother,' Mhatre said, before hanging up.

16

'You should have seen Sadanand's face,' Rohit said, chuckling. Rupa smiled at him.

'You seem to hate him?' she said.

Rohit shrugged.

'Hate would be too strong a word,' he said. 'But till my mother died, he seemed to regard me as a good-for-nothing, and talked to me in a really nasty tone.'

'But you were lagging behind, right? Physics was never your strong subject. That's how he is with all the poor performers.'

'That's because I hated it! I still do.'

'I get that, Rohit. But it's a compulsory subject. And as long as you have to do something …'

'Why not do it well. I remember. My mother used to say the same thing.'

Rupa smiled at him again.

'Which is why I sat up late last night and finished the assignment despite not really wanting to. Only because you insisted. We could have spent some more time here instead.'

Rupa shook her head.

'You needed to finish that assignment,' she said. 'And I'm not going away. Anywhere. Ever.'

Rohit looked at her and grinned. He loved it when she said that.

'Why won't you let me buy you gifts?' he asked.

'I don't need gifts,' she said simply. 'I have all I want.'

'A sixteen-year-old boy is all you want?'

She aimed a punch at him. He ducked and laughed.

'You know what I mean,' she said tenderly.

'Believe me, there's nothing else I want from life either,' he told her.

She moved closer to him and placed her head on his shoulder. He snuggled close and laid his head on top of hers.

'Don't you have exams coming up?' she asked presently.

'You'd know, ma'am,' he said.

She laughed. He loved it when she laughed.

Rohit was aware of a marked feeling of dejection as he cycled back home. He had always hated exams. But now he had reason to hate them more.

'You only have three days to prepare, Rohit. You can't spend all your evenings here with me,' she had told him just before they left the beach.

'But I can't help wanting to!' he said desperately,

his voice rising. A small group of children slowed down to stare as they passed.

'Keep your voice down,' she hushed him in a whisper. 'It's only three days. Prepare well for these exams and make up for your past performance. Then we can spend time together again.'

He was about to argue further but she put her finger on his lips.

'Just three days, Rohit,' she cajoled him. 'Stay at home, study well, ace the exams. I'd hate it if you did poorly because you were meeting me instead of studying. I don't want to distract you.'

He kissed her finger. She smiled a little and drew it away.

'Look,' she said. 'Do this for me, and we will go somewhere over the weekend after your exams. Just you and me. I promise.'

That weekend was what Rohit would live for. Two whole days with her, with no one to disturb them. Two days away from this uncaring, uninteresting world and everything in it that he so abhorred.

Still, he thought, *three days without her is going to be hell.*

He drew up outside his house and clamped the lock shut on his bicycle before walking up the stairs and letting himself in with his latchkey.

His father was sitting in a chair in the living room. As Rohit entered, he looked up from the book he was reading.

'I need to go out of station next weekend,' Rohit said to him.

Deepak looked curious.

'Just a trip with ... with some friends,' Rohit added. 'From college.'

Deepak stared at him hard. Rohit could feel the sweat break out on the back of his neck.

After a long, tense moment, Deepak spoke.

'You need some money for the trip?' he asked.

Rohit shook his head.

'I have some saved up. From what you give me every month. I'll be fine.'

Deepak nodded.

'There's food in the kitchen,' he said.

In his mind, he was thinking, *He's lying*.

17

'You bloody whores, who was it?!'

She sat on the floor of the inner room as Mallik stalked through the lobby of the brothel, rage on his face and a dagger in his hand.

The other women cowered with fear as their pimp paced the room, brandishing the dagger dangerously close to their faces. It was a small lobby to begin with, and Mallik's menacing presence made it seem smaller.

'One of my men ... MY MEN ... was murdered in the alley at the back of this whorehouse, and one of you bitches did it. Now tell me who it was or I'll start cutting you up, one by one, right here. I'll carve your face up so badly that no man will ever touch you again. You'll fucking starve to death!'

She wasn't called Chhaya yet. That name she would earn later. But that morning, after she had taken a life for the first time to save herself from getting raped in the dark alley, she had been too numb to even tell anyone her name.

One of the prostitutes, who had heard the commotion from the window, had come out through the backdoor to check, and found her, partly buried under the henchman's heavy body, half soaked in blood. Hurriedly, she helped her up and took her in, pushing her straight to the bathroom. Only too familiar with the henchman and his lustful ways, the prostitutes rallied around her, bathing her, giving her fresh clothes to wear and feeding her.

All of them knew the consequences would come fast. It was only a matter of time before the body was discovered, and then Mallik would come storming in, armed with that dagger with the long serrated blade.

By the time he did, Rekha, the one who had taken her in, had ushered her into a secret room that was used to hide contraband when the police raided the place. Rekha had made her swear she would not come out for any reason.

The unlicensed brothel was tucked away in a corner of Grant Road, something that Rekha had told her the previous night, and she had no idea how she managed to walk that far. She had lost sense of time since the previous day.

'Who wants to talk?' Mallik asked, his voice suddenly sounding dangerously low.

He grabbed one of them by the hair.

'You?' he asked, bringing the dagger up. 'Want to tell me who killed Daftari? Huh?'

Without warning, he drove the point of the blade into the woman's cheek. She screamed. So did a couple of others.

Rekha stepped forward.

'Mallik! Stop this madness! None of us knows anything, I swear to you!'

Mallik started carving a slow path down the woman's face, as she continued to scream in pain.

'Mallik, stop!'

Rekha lunged for him. He flung the woman to the ground and clutched her by the throat.

'Or what?' he snarled in her face.

They all heard the impact before they saw what happened. In the split second of silence that followed Mallik's last words, they heard something hard and blunt connecting with bone, and the unmistakeable crunch of bone caving in.

Mallik went down as if someone had suddenly pulled out all the bones from his body. Both his hands fell to his side before he sank to the ground and fell awkwardly. Rekha continued to stand where she was, in shock.

The same young girl who had been shivering with fear when she had taken her in six hours ago was now standing over Mallik's lifeless form. She was holding a crowbar in her hands, its end soaked in blood. Rekha even recognised the crowbar. It was stored in the same room where they had hidden her.

Rekha looked at Mallik for a long time before looking up at the girl.

There was absolutely no expression on her face.

Like it always did, the dream jolted her awake. She had become used to it now. Every dream she had was always a recollection of the events that had shaped her into the deadly assassin that she was today. That day at the brothel, she had learned that she was capable of taking a human life. And as the years passed, she only got better at it.

'Hey,' a gentle voice said from beside her. 'What's wrong?'

Chhaya's first instinct was to stiffen. Then she relaxed, remembering where she was.

The girl lying next to her in bed was fair, small-built and very pretty, with short hair and a tiny mole on her cheek, which added to her sex appeal.

Chhaya, who had gone to sleep nestled in her embrace from behind, turned around and smiled at her in the dark.

'Just a bad dream,' she said.

Sanika Grover reached out and ran a hand over her face.

'There's so much I don't know about you ...' she said wonderingly.

Chhaya snuggled even closer to her.

'And yet, here I am, in your house, in bed with you,' she whispered.

Sanika, who knew Chhaya as Jolene Alva, giggled.

'Stop making it sound so scary,' she said and kissed Chhaya on the lips.

They had met two days earlier in the gym and had hit it off instantly. The usually shy Sanika found herself on cloud nine on learning that the new member of her gym, who was so attractive and mysterious at the same time, was a lesbian, like herself. They ended up in bed the next day—Sanika's bed, as she stayed closer to the gym—and this evening, Chhaya had turned up at her place with a bottle of wine.

'Sorry I woke you up,' Chhaya said, running her fingers through Sanika's hair.

'It's okay. You seem to be a restless sleeper. I noticed that last night as well.'

Chhaya smiled again.

'That obvious?' she asked.

Sanika didn't smile back.

'You have bad dreams often?' she asked.

Chhaya paused before answering.

'More often than I'd like to,' she said dispassionately.

This part was true.

Sanika drew Chhaya close and rested her face against her breast.

'It's okay, she said again, rubbing her own face against Chhaya's hair. 'We all have our demons.'

Sanika knew this wasn't permanent. Chhaya had made it clear that she was only on a short visit to the city, to handle some family business. But Sanika was just happy to be with someone who seemed to understand her. Even in 2019, it wasn't exactly easy to be homosexual in India, especially for a woman. Men seemed to view it as an open invitation for perverted and predatory behaviour. Add to that the search for a like-minded companion: always along a thorny path.

As a result, she had to content herself with temporary companionships whenever she was lucky enough to find them. She had tried dating apps, but having sex with someone without any emotional connection whatsoever did not appeal to her.

Sanika suspected that part of her new lover's appeal was how little she knew about her, and how she seemed to be discovering new things about her every time she met her. It had been a while since she had been in a good old-fashioned romance with a stranger.

Another thing about her lover Sanika didn't know was that she was only part of Chhaya's current mission, and that, in a week's time, Chhaya would disappear forever.

Or something much worse would happen.

18

Mhatre hadn't thought it was possible, but ever since Bhatia had resurfaced, his memories of the Shivaji Park incident had intensified. As a result, so had his drinking.

Mhatre was more than a little aware that he was simply using his trauma to fuel his rapidly progressing addiction. But that realisation only came in rare moments of clarity. The rest of the time, he was more than happy to let the inebriation or the resultant hangover numb his feelings.

He was sitting at a cheap tea stall in Antop Hill, sipping some truly terrible coffee, hoping that it would help with the headache.

It didn't.

There was a blank in his memory between the time he had ordered his last drink — or what he remembered to be his last drink — the previous night, and the point where he had found himself struggling to unlock his own door. He had woken up to find his cellphone missing — and located it later under the bed, with absolutely no recollection of how that had happened.

The previous evening, his batchmate Sathe had gone down to Bandstand and joined Sahu in keeping an eye on Ansari. They had watched Ansari and someone who seemed to be his girlfriend for close to an hour, before the couple stood up and got into an auto rickshaw.

Sathe followed the auto on his motorcycle, with Sahu riding pillion, to the Mahim Dargah, where the girl got off. Sathe dropped Sahu off at the dargah as well, and followed Ansari's auto to the Mahim Railway Station, where Ansari boarded a train to Churchgate. When Sathe came back to the dargah, Sahu was standing there, looking lost.

'There were so many women in burqas!' he said helplessly. Sathe looked around and saw his point. A sea of burqa-clad women was constantly entering and exiting at any given point of time. Trying to identify their target was a hopeless case.

Sathe called up Mhatre and told him what had happened. Mhatre told him he understood, told Sahu to go home and then punched his desk in frustration. He had been waiting in the office for the sole purpose of receiving an update from Sahu and Sathe. Everyone else had gone home by then.

Mhatre's phone buzzed as he took another sip of

the coffee. He pulled it out of his pocket and checked the text message from Patankar.

'Lights, camera, action,' the message said. Mhatre had to smile slightly at his reporting head's love of drama.

They were in one of the seediest areas of Antop Hill, spurred by an idea based on something that an instructor at Mhatre's academy had taught him.

That morning, Mhatre had considered his options to try and spur his brain to start working at full capacity.

CDR mapping would only provide rough locations and oblique clues. Interrogation was out of the question right now because of the complaint Siddiqui had submitted. Personal surveillance was not an option for the same reason.

Sathe, or anyone else, would consent to an occasional favour, but no one in the force would spare the resources to put Ansari under surveillance full-time, given the surrounding controversy. Despite his residual popularity following the Shivaji Park incident and the tacit political backing it had won him, Mhatre could not put any other cop in that position.

Think, his instructor at the academy had kept drumming into his head all those years ago. *There are no magic wands in crime detection. No shortcuts, no miracles. The solution is always in your brain, and all you need to do is find it. The trick is to identify that one road you haven't yet taken.*

As he struggled to think past the throbbing in his head, one thing did occur to him. Owing to the whole shebang started by Ansari, he had completely lost sight of the original mission. The case he was investigating was not Ansari. It was Shekhar Bhatia coming to Mumbai after an absence of five years. Bhatia, the facilitator said to have contacts in ordnance factories, who could get you any weapon you needed as long as you paid his price.

Mhatre's mind circled around and then settled on that one operative word.

Weapons. If Bhatia had come to Mumbai, it was to facilitate the delivery of arms. The kind that was much more sophisticated and effective than your average cottage-industry ammunition.

The last time, it had been a military issue grenade that was lobbed at Chintan Mehta at Shivaji Park. What would it be this time?

He found Patankar waiting for him at the squad office.

'You look like hell,' was the first thing his boss said.

Mhatre only nodded. He felt like hell too.

'Good hunch, though. I've sent constables to pick up three of them. Want to go get the fourth?'

'I can't wait to, sir,' Mhatre said.

While the general public is always fascinated by how the police manage to get their information, often it is just the matter of asking the right people. The 'asking' process might not always be polite, but any big crime always has multiple players involved—and at least one of them invariably talks.

Mhatre's hunch was based on simple logistics. The very fact that Bhatia had come to Mumbai indicated that he was working on something big. His record was testament to the fact that he specialised in supplying sophisticated weaponry. But he himself would not bring the weapons to the city—that was not how he worked. It was one of the ways he ensured deniability.

During their phone call in the morning, Patankar and Mhatre had identified four history-sheeters who specialised in smuggling contraband in and out of the city. That included drugs, red sandalwood and endangered species of animals that were in high demand on the black market.

One of them, Gurdeep Singh, was in the transport business, which he used as a front for his smuggling activities. This was the one that Patankar and Mhatre planned to pick up.

And so, here he was, at a tea stall in Antop Hill, two buildings away from Singh's house, while Patankar, in a civilian car, was keeping vigil at the entrance to it, having parked across the lane.

Patankar's message had signified that Singh was on the move. Quickly, he drained his uninspiring cup of coffee, slipped some money under the cup and stood up.

Intersections

He strolled with marked carelessness towards Singh's house, just in time to see the history-sheeter get into his car and start it. He didn't have to ask Patankar what to do next. They had done it countless times before.

As he crossed the street, he heard Patankar start up his own vehicle. He approached Singh's SUV from behind, and just as Singh was about to pull onto the road, he drew abreast and tapped on the front window on the driver's side.

Singh looked to his right with mild irritation. Then his eyes widened.

Mhatre swore under his breath. Apparently, the popularity that had come with the Shivaji Park incident had stuck to him longer than he thought it would. Singh had clearly recognised him.

Mhatre reached behind him and whipped out the gun tucked in his waistband. At the same instant, Singh stepped on the accelerator.

Mhatre was thrown to the side, landing hard on the pavement, as Singh's SUV shot forward. But seconds later, he heard the sound of brakes screeching.

He picked himself up to see Singh's vehicle at a standstill in the middle of the road, half turned to its left. In its path was a truck that had emerged suddenly from an adjoining lane.

Even as Mhatre was regaining his bearings, Patankar, who had exited his car, came running, gun in hand, wrenched open the front passenger door of Singh's SUV, reached across the seat, and unfastened his safety belt. Roughly, Patankar caught hold of Singh's collar and dragged him out of the vehicle, just as Mhatre came running up, his own gun raised.

Even as people on the road began to gather and stare, two uniformed constables with the Antop Hill Police Station, that Patankar had requested beforehand for backup, joined them and started pushing the crowd back.

Patankar shoved Singh into the backseat of his own car, while Mhatre got in beside him, put one arm around his shoulder and shoved the barrel of his pistol firmly into his stomach with the other hand.

'Escape cars in Mumbai only work in movies, bhai,' Mhatre said as Patankar got behind the wheel. 'Nobody told you that?'

'We have a winner, Uday,' Patankar said from the front seat, putting the car into gear.

'Do we, sir?' Mhatre asked.

'Oh, yes,' Patankar replied. 'This man risked injuring a policeman in order to get away. He's hiding something, and he's clearly scared of being found out. Scared of someone more than he is scared of us.'

19

Interrogations are broadly classified into two categories.

The first one is when the suspect is thrown into a room and allowed to sweat for an hour or more, before the cops, with their meanest expressions, barge in and start hurling questions and abuses at the same time. This method works wonders for those who are inside a police lock-up for the first time. First, the waiting, and then, the verbal onslaught, with more than the occasional blow or slap thrown in, work wonders in extracting a confession.

For obvious reasons, this was not going to work with Gurdeep Singh.

The second method is calmer, although it does come with its own moments where a slap is thrown in because the suspect refuses to see sense. It is mostly reserved for history-sheeters who, having faced the system several times, know how it works and also know there are a few ways to beat it.

Hollywood has for long portrayed the second kind of interrogation, where the cops calmly walk into a closed interrogation room with a mirrored wall, laying the suspect's already long record in front of him and telling him to cooperate or get thrown into a supermax facility.

While the Indian police infrastructure has not yet been able to afford sleek interrogation rooms with mirrored walls, going instead for the innermost room of the police station or unit, the method is largely the same. A surprising number of suspects are willing to calmly answer questions put to them by the police—another thing that the movies always get wrong—and hash out their options to get out of the situation with as little damage as possible.

Singh, having been arrested several times in the past and convicted for smuggling twice, was well aware of where he stood. Which is why, when Patankar and Mhatre walked into the room, he merely shifted his position on the cold, hard floor on which they had made him sit, and which was decidedly uncomfortable.

Both the cops drew up chairs and brought their faces as close to their detainee's as they could, without actually touching him.

'Look, bhai,' Patankar said in a reasonable tone. 'You have already been convicted twice, and we now have a clear case of assault on a government servant merely discharging his duty.'

Intersections

Assaulting a government servant had such a broad definition in the Indian Penal Code that the Mumbai Police was in love with that section of the law.

'Plus,' Mhatre added, casually crossing his legs, 'there's that thing that happened in Virar two months ago.'

For the first time, Singh's impassive mask of indifference slipped.

'Oh, yes,' Patankar said. 'You know all about that, don't you?'

'Sir ...' Singh spoke for the first time after being picked up. 'I really have no idea what you are talking about, sir.'

Patankar shook his head, as if in disapproval of Singh's denial.

'Chal, let's humour you,' Mhatre said. 'Two months ago, a truck was stopped by the Virar Police for a routine search on the Mumbai–Ahmedabad Highway. The constable went around the back and found what looked like a tonne of cocaine inside. But before anyone could react, the driver crashed through the barricade and sped away. The constable fell off and was badly injured. As was an officer manning the barricade. They've registered a case of attempt to murder against the driver.'

Singh's face was changing with every word Mhatre uttered.

'We have it on good authority,' Patankar finished, 'that it was one of your trucks.'

'Arrey, sir! What are you saying! My men would never do something like that!'

Patankar and Mhatre both shrugged.

'Like we're going to take *your* word for it, saale,' Patankar said.

'What we are going to do instead is,' Mhatre chimed in, 'arrest you in our case first and then hand you over as a suspect to the Virar Police. After two months of searching, they're going to be more than happy to get their hands on a suspect.'

'What …' Singh began, but then changed tack. 'You can't do that, sir. That's illegal.'

'That's for the court to decide, my friend,' Mhatre said. 'The Virar Police will seek your custody, and given your record, and especially given the fact that you put my life in danger to escape a simple, routine questioning, the court will see merit in their plea. Simple.'

'Very simple,' Patankar added.

Singh was sweating.

'What …' he swallowed. 'What do you want?' he finally asked through gritted teeth.

'Shekhar Bhatia,' Patankar said instantly. Singh slumped, all the fight gone out of him.

Any good cop knows that this is the moment when your suspect, confronted with the knowledge that you know something, has finally broken. Singh's body language in itself was indicative of the fact that he knew something about why Bhatia had come to Mumbai.

'Start talking, Singh,' Mhatre said menacingly. 'We don't have much time before we have to officially declare you detained. Whatever you tell us before that will help you.'

Singh took a deep breath.

'I have one request,' he said.

'Do we look like we're taking requests?' Mhatre snapped.

'Please,' Singh said. 'Just do this much for me.'

Patankar and Mhatre exchanged glances.

'What is it,' Patankar said.

'Arrest me,' Singh said. 'Keep me in the lock-up for a few days. I'll even go to the Virar Police's custody, but I swear to you by everything I regard holy that it wasn't my truck that was involved in that incident in Virar.'

Patankar and Mhatre already knew this. Simply because there had been no incident in Virar two months ago. Their bluff had worked beautifully. And as Singh was neither under arrest not technically even detained, nothing about this conversation was official yet.

'Start talking,' Patankar said. 'Let us see what you have.'

Singh began to talk.

'Bhatia ... he called me a month ago. Told me he needed my services for a special delivery. Didn't tell me the specifics. Just that I needed to keep one vehicle free to transport a medium-size duffel bag in complete secrecy. He didn't even tell me the pick-up point. Said he would tell me exactly a day in advance and I would have two days to deliver it to him after that. And that he would receive it personally.'

'Where?'

'Here. In Mumbai.'

'Are you really saying he didn't tell you what it was?' Mhatre asked.

Singh shook his head.

'I got the sense that it was really important to him. And the payment was unusually good. He offered me a lakh.'

Patankar and Mhatre stared at Singh.

'One lakh for a simple small delivery?'

'And for complete silence on my part. Including with the police. Lifelong.'

'But you're talking to us now.'

'Well, he's disappeared,' Singh said. 'There's been no contact with him for the last one week. And the number I had for him is no longer in service. I'm assuming the job is off. In any case, you picked me up in full public view and word will have got out by now, so I'm definitely off the job even if it is still on.'

Neither cop saw any reason to tell Singh that Bhatia was most likely dead.

Intersections

'If the job is off,' Patankar asked, 'why are you still scared?'

Singh said nothing. Mhatre made a show of examining his face at close quarters.

'You're on a good streak here, Singh,' he said. 'Now is not the time to try our patience.'

Singh still hesitated before speaking again.

'There was this woman present at my meeting with Bhatia ... we only met that once ... she never said a word and was wearing a burqa the entire time. But just before we left, Bhatia drew me aside and told me she'd kill me if I ever breathed a word to anyone.'

'And you believed him?'

'Sir, Bhatia himself is a very dangerous man. And I could see that he takes this woman very seriously. I have no idea who she was, but if she can make Shekhar Bhatia take her seriously, then she scares me.'

Before either Mhatre or Patankar could react, there was a knock on the door.

'Who is it?' Patankar snapped.

The door opened and API Sushmita Kadam stuck her head inside.

'Why is this Chintan Mehta calling you?' she asked Mhatre, holding up his phone, which he had placed on his desk before going into the interrogation.

'Chintan Mehta? The millionaire businessman?'

'How do I know? I only saw the name on the caller ID,' Kadam said, rolling her eyes and passing his phone to him. 'He's called thrice. Better call him back before he comes in here and distributes new cellphones to us all, or something.'

Patankar chuckled. Mhatre took the phone, frowning.

'Wait,' he said. 'What's the date today?'

'July 17,' Patankar and Kadam said in unison.

Mhatre's frown deepened into a scowl.

20

'I will owe you forever for this,' Rekha, the woman Chhaya had saved, said sincerely.

'Not at all, darling,' Shekhar Bhatia said, sitting comfortably on the worn-out sofa which, at night, was used by clients as they sat sipping their drinks and choosing their girl for the night from the line-up.

After Chhaya had bludgeoned Mallik to death, Rekha had phoned the only person she knew who could handle a situation like this. Bhatia had been a client of hers for a little over a year. Despite the fact that he made more than enough money, he still liked to frequent seedy brothels tucked away in the corners of Grant Road, well away from the bustle and noise of Kamathipura. He had told her that the high-priced call girls there, with sophistication and confidence oozing out of their pores, made him nervous. Bhatia had taken a liking to Rekha and she knew she could depend on him.

Rekha also knew that Bhatia moved in the shadier circles of power, and that if anyone could get the brothel out of this mess, it was him.

True enough, he had listened to her patiently and told her he would be there within the hour, adding that no one there should touch anything. When he arrived, he was accompanied by three burly men, one of them carrying a large duffel bag.

Quickly, efficiently and silently, they removed sheets of tarpaulin from the bag, wrapped up Mallik's body, tied it with hemp rope and stuffed it into the bag. Two of them carried the bag outside, while the third supervised the prostitutes as they scrubbed the floor clean of Mallik's blood with soap water. Bhatia just sat on the couch, smoking a cigarette.

When it was all done, Bhatia took Rekha aside and slipped her a large envelope.

'There's enough cash in this to see you through for a month. Get out of the city today. I can't help the other girls, but tell them to run away as well. Mallik's employers are not going to take kindly to his disappearance, let alone his murder,' he said in a low voice.

'I can't leave the rest of them on their own,' a trembling Rekha protested.

'Yes, you can. Look, I'd take you with me right now, but I'm already taking the girl because you asked – she still hasn't said a word, by the way. I can't manage the two of you at the same time. I should be back in a month and I'll call you then. Please do as I say.'

Bhatia turned to the girl.

'Time to leave,' he said, smiling at her. 'Don't worry. You're going to be safe.'

Intersections

She looked at him, expressionless, before standing up. He walked to the door and she followed him without saying anything. At the door, she stopped and turned around to look at Rekha. She held her gaze for a long moment, then nodded once, turned around and left.

'That girl is not human,' a prostitute whispered to Rekha.

'She's had to kill two people in less than a day — and we don't even know what she went through before this happened,' Rekha answered. 'If there ever was a human being alive inside her, there isn't one anymore.'

Bhatia and the girl exited through the same back door, leading into the same alley where she had taken a life for the first time. A car was waiting and there was no sign of the three men that Bhatia had brought with him.

'Come,' Bhatia said, sliding into the driver's seat. She got into the passenger seat. Silently, they drove all the way to the Lokhandwala Complex in Andheri, where a flat had been readied for her beforehand.

'There's money and enough supplies for a month,' Bhatia told her. 'I have to go out of the country for at least a month. Anything you need, I've saved a number in the cellphone in the bedroom. The owner of that number will come to check on you regularly. Speak to no one but him.'

She nodded.

'You need a doctor?' he asked.

She shook her head.

'Okay.'

Bhatia turned to leave.

'Thank you.'

It startled Bhatia a bit. He had grown used to her not speaking, and hearing her voice for the first time felt strange. She too realised that it was the first time she had spoken in two days.

'Don't ... don't worry about it. If things go smoothly, I'll be back soon,' Bhatia said, then walked out and shut the door behind him.

Chhaya was brought back to the present by the sound of another door shutting.

'I'm home!' Sanika called out. She was an investment banker, and her work timings were one reason why Chhaya had chosen her as an unwitting accessory.

She came out of the kitchen, smiling, reminding herself that her name was supposed to be Jolene.

'What smells so good?' Sanika asked, slipping into a chair and kicking her shoes off. Chhaya had tried heels only once. She found them completely impractical and had no idea why anyone would want to wear them on a daily basis.

'I ordered some chicken steaks from this place I found on Swiggy,' Chhaya said, moving behind Sanika's chair and placing her hands on her friend's shoulders. 'They come pre-marinated, so I only had to grill them. We can make a quick salad to go with them.'

Sanika closed her eyes as Chhaya began massaging her shoulders.

'An interior designer who makes delicious smelling steaks and massages like a pro. Exactly how many more skills are you hiding from me, Jolene Alva?' she asked.

Chhaya leaned down and kissed Sanika on the top of her head.

'You haven't seen the half of it, Sanika Grover,' she whispered. Sanika smiled, her eyes still closed.

'Want some wine?' Chhaya asked.

'Later. After a shower.'

'I'll start on the salad, then.'

'You're an angel.'

Later, they flopped into easy chairs at a window of Sanika's fourth-floor apartment, with a clear view of Girgaum Chowpatty across the street. Sanika had a glass of red wine in her hand, while Chhaya was sipping a soda. She had never seen any reason to numb her senses with intoxicants.

'When did you realise it?' Sanika asked, looking at the lights in the distance.

'Realise what?' Chhaya asked.

'That you preferred women?'

Chhaya's mind flashed back to the time Rekha had stripped and bathed her, and how her touch had made her feel comfortable and safe.

'I was quite young when I first started feeling a hint of it,' she said. 'But it took me years to process it.'

'Same here,' Sanika said. 'You don't just wake up and see a sign one morning. You struggle with the feeling, especially with all the guilt that the world likes to heap on it. I lived in denial for years before it all got too much and I came out to my parents.'

'How did they take it?'

Sanika gave a short laugh.

'My father tried to strangle me in my sleep that night. I left home the next day.'

Chhaya reached out and laid her hand on Sanika's.

'I'm so sorry.'

'It's okay. It only cemented my belief that men are vile beasts.'

Chhaya thought of Daftari, the enforcer who tried to rape her in the alley, and Mallik, who used to pimp for a living and was ready to carve women's faces up if they didn't obey his every word.

She also thought of the other men she had killed.

'Absolute beasts,' she said.

Sanika drained her glass.

'You want to eat?' she asked. Chhaya understood. She knew from personal experience that not everyone liked to dwell too long on the traumas of the past.

'Sure. I'm starving,' she said, standing up.

Sanika stood, too, and took her glass from her before going to the kitchen.

Before following her, Chhaya took one last look out of the window and at the spot where her target was going to be exactly a week from now.

21

Mhatre was decidedly uncomfortable, and the fact that he had gone to sleep — or tried to — without drinking the previous night was only half the reason. He had slept so little that he was running on fumes and two cups of black coffee this morning.

He was sitting on a chair put up on a temporary stage at Shivaji Park, with Chintan Mehta next to him. There was a huge crowd in front of him, and he could feel his legs shaking a bit. Contrary to what his detractors said behind his back about his so-called sudden fame going to his head, the attention actually made him very uneasy.

It had surprised him that he had forgotten the date, with all that had been going on recently, till Mehta had called him up the previous day to remind him. For the last four years, he had never needed to be reminded of this date.

July 18 was the day that the attack on Chintan Mehta had changed his life forever. While the media quickly came to call it the 'Shivaji Park incident', for

Mhatre it remained an attack on innocent civilians caught in the middle of a crowd. Someone had snuck in a military-issue grenade and used it, and killed five people in the process. The incident was a reminder of just how fragile life could be.

Every year after the incident, the news media would do stories about its anniversary, as if it were an event to be celebrated and to remind people about. Articles would be written and television segments would be run on how the victims' families were getting on and how they were coping with their irreparable loss. Reporters would flock to get a soundbite from Mehta. Mhatre, being the hero who gunned the assassin down, naturally came under the spotlight as well.

After the first year, Mhatre had requested the police commissioner to grant him leave on the anniversary of the incident in subsequent years. The commissioner had refused, saying that he understood Mhatre's emotions but, whether he liked it or not, he was the face of the Mumbai Police as far as the attack was concerned.

Mhatre looked down at the crowd seated in chairs in front of the dais. The front row was occupied by the families of the five victims. He saw Shireen's parents, Reema's parents and elder sister, Sehar's parents, Vasant's wife and two sons and Ashok's brother. All of them seemed to have aged by several years after the incident. Mhatre knew that the void that had been left in their lives after that afternoon five years ago had slowly been sucking the life out of them.

Chief Minister Chandrakant Waghmare finished his rehearsed and predictable speech about strength and resilience and the spirit of the city, and returned to his seat on the dais. The compere then announced Mehta's name. He stood up, as one used to such things, and took the mic. Mhatre had politely refused to speak this year, and Mehta, with some reluctance, had agreed.

'Those who know me also know that oration isn't exactly my strong suit,' began Mehta on a suitably humble note. 'Also, we have politicians here and I wouldn't dream of trying to beat them at their own game.' The crowd chuckled. Mhatre did too. Mehta genuinely seemed to have no fear of the political lobby.

'But the honourable chief minister wanted me to be the one to make this announcement today, and like any good businessman, I need to keep the political leadership happy.'

There was laughter again. Waghmare himself applauded the humour of his address, laughing all the while in appreciation. Mhatre was willing to bet that Waghmare had been briefed beforehand on everything that Mehta was going to say to regale the crowd.

'What happened outside this very ground five years ago was not only an attempt on my life,' he said more soberly, 'it was also an attempt at disrupting the peace in our country, in our state and our city, by elements based beyond our borders. I am told that certain members of the criminal underworld, who I, like many other businessmen, refuse to bow down to, wanted me to die a very public death.'

Mhatre listened intently. Like all successful businessmen, Mehta had received his share of extortion calls. Mhatre and Patankar had spent all their energies probing the case around the attack on Mehta, but with the assassin dead and no concrete proof linking him to Bhatia, there had simply been no definite leads.

Ultimately, a vague report was passed down by central intelligence agencies, according to which 'activity' in a neighbouring country, where a fugitive gangster was supposed to be based, had increased in the days leading up to the incident. Based on the report, a formal FIR was filed against the gangman and, because he was based beyond the country's borders, the case was handed over to the National Investigation Agency for further inquiry. The case remained unsolved till date and Mhatre suspected that the whole gangster angle was just a convenient sham, although he would never be able to say it out loud.

'But if they want to hit out at us,' Mehta went on, 'we will hit back. One week from now, Chief Minister Waghmare and I are inaugurating a whole new fleet of patrol boats at Girgaum Chowpatty. I have played a minor part in the funding of the project. This much you already know.'

Mehta paused to let this sink in, before going on.

'I would also like to announce today that, at the same function, I will be handing over a cheque for one crore rupees, to be used to double the number of CCTV cameras in the city.'

The crowd broke out into spontaneous applause, which went on for a good three to four minutes.

'Because we are not savages like those gangsters are, our best offence is a good defence. We will make the city so secure that no one will even be able to look at it with evil intentions in their eyes.'

The crowd roared their approval and another spell of applause followed, with Waghmare and Mhatre both standing up to clap. As the cheering died down, Mehta concluded his speech.

'Sorry about that clichéd ending. It was the best I could do, with my limited skills,' he said, walking off amidst continued congratulations.

The function ended with a vote of thanks, after which Mhatre went with Mehta to his car. As it was an official appearance, Mhatre was in uniform, his gun nestling snugly in his hip holster. As he had known it would, the walk from the ground to Mehta's car triggered a flood of memories, and his hand automatically went to his holster.

Mehta noticed this as they came to a stop near the rear door of his car, the engine already idling.

'Get in for a minute,' Mehta said, smiling. Mhatre went around and climbed in beside him. 'I heard about the complaint against you,' Mehta said, and Mhatre's eyes flew to the driver in the front seat. Mehta waved to indicate that he could be trusted.

'No one said it was going to be easy, right?' Mhatre said, grinning.

'How are you doing, Mr Mhatre? Honestly?'

Mhatre looked away, out of the window.

'You know my problem with superhero stories, Mr Mehta?' he asked.

'Do tell.'

'The hero gets these fantastic powers that allow him to do great things. Move matter with his mind, fly, punch through steel and concrete, see through walls. You name it. And what does he do? He spends the first half of the story being scared of his powers and whining about how he is not ready for the responsibility. He absolutely insults the privilege that he has. Agreed, every superhero's powers come at the cost of great personal tragedy. But once you have the powers, is it really right to disrespect them like that?'

Mehta took a second before responding.

'So ... you don't like superheroes?'

'I don't like their attitude,' Mhatre replied. 'What happened here five years ago gave me a certain power.

The fame opened many doors for me. Political backing gave me a chance to do some real good work. The reputation of someone who will not hesitate to pull the trigger if you try his patience was instrumental in loosening the tongues of countless criminals in lock-up. All I am doing is ensuring that I use all of that to do my job.'

Mehta nodded.

'You're respecting your powers,' he said.

'I'm trying my best,' Mhatre said, finally turning around to look at Mehta. 'Because if one more innocent person dies on my watch, it will be that turning point in the story where the superhero loses sense of right and wrong and sets the world on fire.'

22

API Sushmita Kadam slipped another lozenge into her mouth and reached for her touchpad.

Sliding her fingers over it, she tapped on another video and started watching it intently.

It had taken a phone call from DCP Samad Khan, but the control room had finally sent the CCTV camera footage that the squad had asked for.

It was one of the most tedious jobs in crime detection, but it also yielded dividends in terms of clues. Kadam remembered the first time she had worked with CCTV footage and how impressed she had been with the results it afforded her.

She had been with the Sion Police Station at the time, a PSI on the brink of promotion. The case was a routine one, and one of the most common crimes in the jurisdiction. Two men on a bike had slowed down near a housewife on her way home from the local market, snatched the solid gold chain she was wearing, and sped away.

Normally, it would have been impossible to catch the thieves, simply because they would be long gone by the time the woman reached the police station. In this case, two beat constables on a routine patrol saw it happen and started giving chase while simultaneously calling it in.

Kadam, who was in the police station, heard it and saw an officer, with two more constables, rush to the nearest vehicle to give chase. They didn't even look at her. She was, after all, a woman. Modernisation and gender sensitisation workshops notwithstanding, the fact that a woman should be part of a chase is never the first thought to cross the minds of the male majority of the police force.

As the patrolling constables repeated the location and the descriptions of the two men—they were too far behind to see the licence plate as yet—she jotted them down. Bikes are the getaway vehicles of choice for chain-snatchers, because of the speed and mobility they afford, as opposed to four-wheelers. There is the added fact that very few policemen ride their bikes as recklessly as chain-snatchers do.

Kadam thought for a second and then called the control room. Quickly, she told the officer who answered what she needed, and hinted that she would owe him a favour if he helped her out. He called her back ten minutes later, even as the policemen chasing the chain-snatchers called in on the wireless, saying they had lost the suspects.

Kadam wrote down what the control room officer told her, and then went to the senior inspector's cabin.

'The chain-snatchers we're looking for?' she said. 'They've just turned into the Eastern Express Highway, near Ghatkopar.'

'And you know this, how?' her reporting head asked.

'I called the control room with their description and location, and they tracked them through CCTV live feed. They're still doing it, and if we ask the Vikhroli Police to divert their nearest units ...'

The senior inspector immediately reached for his wireless and at the next monthly crime conference, Kadam was lauded in front of all the attending senior officers. Patankar, who was present at the conference, put in a word with the higher-ups, and when Kadam's promotion came in, she was posted to the Zone I squad.

While Mhatre and Mehta were at Shivaji Park, and Patankar was in his cabin—no doubt butchering another song—Kadam and three constables from the squad were examining footage from some thirty cameras from the day of the Sitaara Hotel fire. They had started with the ones around the hotel first and, as soon as they spotted Bhatia and the woman in the burqa, started reverse tracking their movements.

It took hours, but by the end of it, one thing was clear. The woman had never taken off her burqa, not even once. They were still nowhere on her identity.

Intersections

Their movements, however, had been interesting.

As the attendant at Sitaara Hotel had told Mhatre, Bhatia and the woman had checked in at eleven in the morning. Reverse tracking with the help of other CCTV cameras established that they had come on foot, with only a single duffel bag between them. That bag, half-burned, was now in the custody of the MRA Marg police, and had been found to contain only clothes.

Next, Kadam and her team checked the footage from the CST Station and spotted them leaving the station half an hour earlier. Kadam took a second to think before her next step. There were any number of railway stations from where they could have taken the train to get to CST. Getting footage of the stations from all the concerned police units would itself take a month. She went to Patankar's cabin and told him what she needed. He agreed and picked up his phone.

Once again, Patankar thought about how technology had changed the process of crime detection.

He opened his WhatsApp application and accessed a group that had all police inspectors and senior inspectors in charge of police stations or units, including those heading railway police stations. He started typing out a message, addressing specifically the railway police station heads, seeking help with locating Shekhar Bhatia on their respective CCTV camera networks. He also sent a still of Bhatia, the clearest that Kadam could find, captured on a camera outside the CST Station.

He hit send and placed his phone aside. No one would acknowledge his message, but everyone would see it and those concerned would do the needful. It was a pre-established protocol to not respond with acknowledgements, simply because it would create an unnecessary flood of messages saying 'ok' or 'sure' on the group.

It wasn't as if the police did not have enough unchecked notifications on their phone through the day in the first place, including some completely unwanted forwarded jokes and videos. Almost every policeman that Patankar knew had, like him, turned off the media auto download feature on WhatsApp. The sheer number of funny videos, not to mention 'good morning' and 'goodnight' images forwarded by civilians eager to fraternise would make any cellphone give up the ghost within a day.

Mhatre walked in five minutes later, looking tired.

'How did it go?' Patankar asked.

'The usual. You heard about Mehta's announcement, I presume?'

Patankar nodded. 'I really can't figure him out,' he said. 'He pours crores of rupees into social work every year. The tax relief must be massive. But all of this only to save a few lakh rupees in tax?'

Mhatre grinned. 'And they call *me* a cynic,' he said.

'I might be wrong,' Patankar acknowledged. 'But no one is ever that pure and altruistic.'

'Pure? I don't think he's pure. I'm sure there are many skeletons buried under the road that led to his current riches. But right now, he's doing good work, right?

'That's exactly my point. Is he simply doing good work or is he atoning for something? Because if he is, what makes a man so guilty as to spend enough money to finance a small country in Africa?'

'And now you've spoiled his image in my eyes.' Mhatre sighed exaggeratedly.

Kadam popped her head inside. She was holding another bunch of papers.

Patankar looked up and Mhatre looked around to see that she was smiling.

'The number that Bhatia was using—we got its CDRs,' she said.

23

The man with the salt-and-pepper hair and beard slipped a bookmark into the novel he was reading, closed it and slid it into his shoulder-bag. Unhurriedly, he took off his reading glasses, folded them and placed them inside their case, which, too, went into the bag. He was dressed in a simple shirt and jeans, and seemed to be totally detached from everything around him.

Across the aisle, a young man stood up and picked up the paper bag he had with him. He was handling it with great care, the older man noticed.

Just as the train entered CST, the older man stood up, slung his bag over his shoulder and walked to the door. There were few other passengers in the train.

The young man, eager to get off early, edged himself in front of the older man. As the train started slowing down, he shuffled forward, only to feel a restraining hand on his shoulder.

'Wait,' the older man behind him said in a deep voice. His grip was inoffensive but firm.

Intersections

The young man decided to surrender himself to it. As the train started slowing down, men and women waiting on the platform started jumping aboard, brushing, even pushing past the two. The older man held on to his shoulder till the crowd thinned out and then let go.

Once the mad rush was over, both men alighted easily, one behind the other. The younger man then turned around.

'Thanks,' he said, and the other man only nodded. Turning, they both headed for the exit of the concourse.

'You know, it's funny,' the young man said, falling into step beside his silent travel companion. 'I had you pegged for a first-timer like myself. You've obviously been in Mumbai before.'

'Not for a long time,' the older man said. 'I'm coming here after ten years.'

'Did the crowd jump in like that ten years ago as well? I mean, the compartment was practically empty and there were still a few seats left after they all got in.'

'Mob mentality is independent of time, or place. Human beings, for the most part, will always want to get everywhere first. This is why we need to teach our kids that not coming first is completely acceptable.'

'Is that what you teach your kids?' the young man asked.

'I don't have kids,' the older man said with a smile.

They stopped at the exit to face each other.

'Anuj Sodhi,' the young man said, offering his hand. 'From Nashik.'

'Oscar Fernandes,' the older man said, closing his firm grip around Anuj's palm. 'From nowhere in particular.'

Anuj chuckled.

'I kind of like that! Maybe I'll use it to impress the girl I'm meeting.'

Oscar looked interested.

'You came from Nashik to Mumbai to meet a girl?'

'It's an arranged marriage meeting,' Anuj said self-consciously. 'We've been talking on the phone for a couple of weeks now. I got to Mumbai last night and am meeting her at a café here.'

'Well, in that case, I'd advise against using that line when you're introducing yourself. She already knows where you're from. And unless you can figure out a good reply when she asks why you said that, it will be awkward as hell.'

Anuj looked sheepish.

'You're … you're right,' he said.

Oscar leaned forward.

'If you have to put on an act to impress her,' he said, 'she's not worth it.'

He let go of Anuj's hand, nodded and walked away, disappearing into the crowd.

As Anuj started looking for a taxi, Oscar made his way out of the station premises and walked to

Intersections

D.N. Road. The street is lined with buildings on both sides, occupied by hundreds of offices of all sorts.

Oscar knew where he was going. He'd been there before. Deftly sidestepping vendors selling a wide range of wares, he ducked into a building on his left and walked up to the first floor. From memory, he turned right and pushed open the third door in the corridor.

'I have an appointment with Mr Deepak Garg,' he told the receptionist inside.

24

In police circles, it is informally known as 'building a theory'.

There comes a point in every investigation when the investigating team gathers enough facts to be able to build a working theory. If nothing else, it helps put the facts into perspective. Legend has it that during the Sheena Bora murder case, the investigating team had built what they thought was a sound theory to work with. Then came the revelation that Sheena was actually the accused Indrani Mukerjea's daughter, and not sister, like the world believed, and the theory was shot to bits.

The pitfall is that there is a dangerously high scope for assumptions, which might colour the facts. Sir Arthur Conan Doyle said it best in his Sherlock Holmes series. *It is a capital mistake to theorise before one has the data. Insensibly, one begins to twist facts to suit theories, instead of theories to suit facts.*

Mhatre, Kadam and Patankar had all agreed that

they had enough facts to go on, and could take the risk of building a primary theory.

'A month ago,' Patankar began the construction, 'Bhatia, using a new cellphone, contacts Gurpreet Singh and engages his services for a delivery to be made at a later date on short notice. Two weeks later, Bhatia, using the same cellphone, contacts Niyaz Ansari. The numbers match in Singh and Ansari's CDRs. I think we can all agree that a job was being planned. Based on their histories, I'd say Bhatia was smuggling a powerful weapon from the ordnance factory and Singh was smuggling it into the city. We don't know exactly what Ansari's role was, but he could have been the receiver once the weapon reached the city.'

Kadam leaned forward and said, 'According to the CDRs of the number that Bhatia was using, the first call that he made came from Punjab. It was his native place and it makes sense that he would relocate there following the heat from the Shivaji Park attack. It was also safe for him to use the number from his hometown, because unless someone was specifically looking for it, no one would make the connection.'

Patankar and Mhatre both nodded.

'Had he not died in that fire, we would not even have come this far in the investigation. Whatever they were planning, that fire seems to have ruined it for them,' Patankar said.

'Is that why the job is off?' Mhatre asked.

'We don't know if it really is off, or if Singh was cut out of the equation for some reason. Maybe Bhatia's death changed something and the woman, assuming she's also part of the plot, decided to go in for a completely new team for reasons of safety.'

'The woman *must* have been part of it. She attended the meeting with Singh, and Bhatia told Singh she'd kill him if he told anyone. She *has* to have been involved.'

'More on that later,' Patankar said. 'Go on,' he said to Kadam.

'Bhatia's CDRs and his movements on CCTV cameras confirm that he arrived in Mumbai a day before the Sitaara Hotel fire. As far as I could tell, he came by train from Punjab to Mumbai and got off at Dadar. He stayed overnight, and also met Singh on that day, according to the results of Singh's interrogation. The next day, he took a cab to Byculla, and seems to have boarded another train to CST.'

'Precautions,' Mhatre said promptly.

'Yes,' Patankar said. 'Mumbai was ground zero and now they had to be very careful. They wanted to make it appear as if they had only just arrived in the city on the day they checked into the Sitaara.'

'Then the fire breaks out,' Mhatre picked up from where Patankar left off, 'Bhatia dies and the woman disappears. Ansari, whom we had picked up, gets that nobody, Tahir Siddiqui, to file a complaint against me, and changes his SIM card.'

'Is that so?' Patankar asked.

'Yes, his old number is no longer active,' Kadam replied. 'I tried getting recent CDRs today and learned that his SIM card stopped functioning the day the complaint was filed with Khan sir.'

'You have the last dialled number?'

'Yes, and I have already asked for its CDRs. His location during the last call he made was the vicinity of his own house. The number he called was located in Bandra.'

Patankar gave her a look of approval. He loved the woman's efficiency.

'Umm ...' Mhatre said. 'Any idea where in Bandra?'

'We'll know from the CDRs. I should have them today. The day is still young,' Kadam said, smiling.

Mhatre smiled back half-heartedly and said nothing.

He looked at Patankar, expecting him to go on. His reporting head, however, was staring at him fixedly, without saying anything.

'What?' Mhatre asked, avoiding his look.

Patankar continued to stare.

'Sir?' Kadam asked, puzzled.

'What are you not telling us?' Patankar asked finally.

Mhatre blinked and looked at Kadam. Patankar followed his eyes and then looked back at him.

'She's as much part of the investigation as we are. I'm not cutting her out of anything,' Patankar said.

Mhatre fidgeted in his seat uncomfortably.

'We're waiting.'

Mhatre sighed. Succinctly, he narrated how he had tasked his informant with trailing Ansari and then sought help from his batchmate in Unit IX. He ended by telling Patankar and Kadam how his informant had lost the woman at the Mahim Dargah.

'You do realise what this means?' Patankar said.

'That the Bandra connection is significant and needs to be looked into?' Mhatre said, looking at his hands.

'No!' Patankar shouted. 'It means we can't officially use this connection because the information was obtained using methods that won't be acceptable in court.'

'Sir ...'

'I know, I know. "We'll manage, we'll find some loophole, we always do." But you're forgetting something. You put a tail on Ansari *after* he had a complaint submitted against you. Any defence lawyer worth his gown is going to tear you, and the entire case, to shreds, using that fact alone. And I don't see any judge not throwing the book at you.'

Intersections

'The system has always—' Mhatre began sourly but Patankar cut him off.

'Are you seriously going to sit there and give me a lecture on how much the system sucks? You think I don't know? You think I haven't seen enough examples? Or do I have to remind you that the very reason why I'm your reporting head is that I've put in more number of years on the job than you have?'

Mhatre said nothing.

'You see my dilemma? The information is crucial. It warrants us to start a focused search for this woman in the Bandra area. Even if she is long gone, there could be some trail. She might have checked into some hotel. There's a chance a CCTV camera might have captured her face, even if she was using some kind of disguise. We have endless possibilities, but to explore them, I have to stand in front of Khan and tell him what you did!'

Kadam tried to edge out of the room. 'I ... I should go check on the CDRs ...'

'No, you will stay here. And you will take note of the fact that I am prepared to take any amount of flak for your sakes, but not if you're going to keep me in the dark. Whatever methods you employ, whatever corners you cut, I want to be in the loop. I can handle surprises, just not from my own people.'

Patankar stood up, drained.

'Khan was right,' he said bitterly to Mhatre. 'You're getting out of control and you don't seem to understand protocol.'

He turned and walked to the door.

'Where are you going, sir?' Kadam asked cautiously.

'To tell Khan about this fucking mess and to beg him to let us pursue this lead further,' Patankar said and stormed out.

25

Anuj checked himself again in the mirror.

He still wasn't sure if he should change his shirt. And he had bought a new pair of shoes, just to impress her. He was debating whether to put them on instead of the sneakers that he usually wore with his shirt and jeans.

Then he remembered Oscar's advice to him at the station and smiled.

I'll just be myself, he thought.

He left his hotel room and went down the stairs. The cab was waiting for him outside.

Hello, Anuj said to himself softly, as they drove away. *I'm Anuj ...*

He stopped and shook his head. She already knew his name. It sounded doubly stupid because he was meeting her for the second time tonight.

The first meeting had gone like a dream. She was way more beautiful than she looked in her pictures, and as they talked, he found himself getting increasingly impressed with her confidence and poise. Before the meeting was over, he knew that he had found the one thing he always looked for in a woman. Intellectual stimulation. He found himself wanting to know more and more about her thoughts.

Hi ... he tried again. *You're looking lovely ...*

He shook his head. It was the oldest and most clichéd compliment in the book.

He wished he had asked for Oscar Fernandes' number so that they could figure out a good opening line together. Then he chortled to himself.

Pretty sure Oscar has more important things to do than play love guru, he thought.

Oscar, in fact, would have loved the distraction.

He had just come back to his hotel after another terribly boring day.

It had been ten years since he had resigned from the Mumbai Police and left the city, vowing to never return if he could help it.

He had some ancestral property in Nagpur that more than took care of his monetary needs. His father had moved from their native Goa a year after he was born because he found that place growing crowded and noisy. After several years of moving around with no fixed address or job, a luxury afforded to his father due to some royalties he had earned as a writer, he had ultimately bought an orchard in Nagpur and decided to settle there.

Intersections

Oscar's job as a policeman had been chosen more out of passion than necessity. Ever since he could remember, he had wanted to be a cop. The career choice was influenced, in no small measure, by his father's description of policemen in his books. The respect that came with the uniform was something he found himself craving for. He started seeing a grown-up version of himself, dressed in a crisp uniform, black sunglasses on his nose, leaving for work on his Enfield motorbike, while everyone looked on with deference.

When he was a teenager, his father moved them to Mumbai as he had the opportunity to convert some of his novels into films. Oscar immediately fell in love with the city, as well as with the Mumbai Police. Those were the days when encounters were at their peak and the idea of putting down dreaded criminals in gunfights appealed to Oscar.

'There is no right or wrong,' his father would often say. 'Whatever solves the problem is right. Whatever doesn't, is wrong.'

For the young Oscar, therefore, executing criminals was right. If they were released from prison, they'd go back to harming society. Execution solved the problem of recidivism.

That changed within a year of his being selected as a police sub-inspector, when he learned that half the encounter killings were actually contract killings for underworld dons, that the force was almost entirely corrupt, and that a majority of the policemen were only in the force for the benefits they got as government servants.

He was twenty-eight when he joined the force. He managed to stay in it till he turned thirty-five, and then, after the incident that changed his life forever, put in his papers and left the city to tend to the orange orchard in Nagpur. Both his parents had died by then.

Shaking his head at the memory, Oscar rummaged around in his trouser pocket till he found his pack of cigarettes and lighter.

As he lit up, he had a feeling he was going to die of boredom on this job.

26

'Where?'

The text message was from Patankar.

Mhatre was already on his third drink and had half a mind to not respond after the way the evening had gone.

After Patankar had left, Kadam stood up and walked out of the room without saying anything. Mhatre kept sitting in his chair, his mind going through a mix of emotions. He knew what Patankar had said was not wrong.

He had heard of enough examples, both during his training and after he joined the force, about entire cases collapsing just because the right procedure was not followed in one small part of the investigation. All the phrases, including 'reasonable doubt', and 'fruit of the poisoned tree', which were thrown around in Hollywood courtroom dramas, held true for the Indian system as well. Mercifully, Bollywood hadn't got its hands on those phrases yet. He shuddered to think what their representation would be in a culture where courtroom thrillers hinged on two lawyers shouting at each other in a crowded courtroom.

At the same time, he also knew that results were not always obtained by following the rule book. He had thought that Patankar, being a Crime Branch veteran and having lived through an era where so many rules were bent so that organised crime could be brought under control, would understand. He had not even known that sending his informant to trail Ansari would yield any results. But now there was a definite link, a fresh one that might even produce some leads about the mystery woman.

He sat brooding for more than an hour before there was a knock on the door of Patankar's cabin. He looked up to see Kadam. She looked uneasy.

'Colaba ACP's office just called. You're to record your statement with him. It's … it's part of the inquiry into the complaint …'

Mhatre nodded. 'Now?' he asked.

'They said, as soon as possible.'

He stood up and went past her, mumbling his thanks, and exited the squad office. The office of the ACP Colaba division, Shankar Deshmukh, was in the same compound. Deshmukh was said to be a good officer—in the sense that he didn't believe in making things unnecessarily difficult for his fellow policemen.

Deshmukh called him inside, his writer sitting across the table from him.

'We'll keep it to the point,' Deshmukh said. 'The complaint submitted by ...' he consulted the copy of the complaint on his desk, '... Tahir Siddiqui says that you flouted the rules while detaining him, Usman Ahmed and Niyaz Ansari. Allegations are that they were assaulted with undue force and kept in detention for more than the prescribed twenty-four hours. Let's keep your statement confined to only these allegations, and before you know it, this will all be over.'

Mhatre smiled gratefully. Deshmukh was telling him that anything else that did not strictly pertain to the specific allegations was not required. Deshmukh also did not want to be put in a position where he was made aware of any facts that he could not ignore, facts that he would then be obligated to make part of the official record. Deshmukh was duty-bound to conduct the inquiry because Khan had told him to. But he would be damned if he was going to give any further ammunition to those three criminal elements to use against his own brethren.

Mhatre took a minute to compose his thoughts. Deshmukh waited patiently, before half-turning to his writer. The post of a 'writer' is assigned to a constable, just like the 'reader'. The writer types the officer's official paperwork in the approved terminology, while the reader peruses all his incoming mail and sorts it in order of priority.

Mhatre outlined how he had received a tip-off about Siddiqui, Ahmed and Ansari being together, and how, due to their antecedents, he had reason to suspect that they were planning a crime together. He went on to state how they were picked up from Dadar and brought to the squad office, and added that he had held them in the Colaba Police Station lock-up for a short while after which he had some other work to take care of. He denied assaulting any of them, and ended by stating that they were released twenty-three hours and thirty minutes after they were brought in.

'Good enough,' Deshmukh said. He turned to the writer. 'Type that out and send it to me for signature right away. Mhatre, will you tell Patankar to come and record his statement as well?'

'Yes, sir,' Mhatre said, standing up and saluting. He had not had much to do with Deshmukh, and this was the longest time that he had spent in the same room with him. But he liked the man already.

He paused before turning to leave.

'Thank you, sir,' he said.

Deshmukh just nodded.

'Patankar sir texted,' Kadam told him as he entered the squad office. 'Khan sir is in some meeting so Patankar sir has to wait. He says we can leave if there's nothing else.'

'You need help with those CDRs?'

'Oh, the fresh ones I'd asked for haven't come in yet. You're going to stay?'

'I have to sign my statement. Shouldn't take long.'

Intersections

Kadam paused for a few seconds.

'You want to have dinner somewhere? My parents are out of town and I don't feel like going home and cooking.'

Mhatre hesitated. It wasn't like he had any prior engagement, but ...

'I'm supposed to meet someone on my way home,' he said, 'a ... a batchmate ...'

'It's okay,' Kadam said quickly, standing up. 'I'll get going, then.'

They both knew he was lying, and that he was going to go and drink.

'Next time?' he said.

She nodded. They both knew he didn't really mean it.

An hour later, having signed his statement and taken a copy, he was at his usual bar.

His phone buzzed again.

'*Abey, bata na, gandu ...*'

Mhatre smiled. Patankar was not mad at him anymore. That was a start.

He replied to the message with the name of the bar. Not a minute later, Patankar slid into the seat in front of him.

Mhatre waited till Patankar ordered a drink for himself.

'How bad is it?' he then asked.

'Khan's not happy, of course. But he's a cop and he knows how important the lead could turn out to be,' Patankar said, picking up his glass and raising it. Mhatre followed suit and they both took a sip.

'So?'

'So he's told us to pursue it, and that we'll see how to present it if it pans out into something worthwhile.

'Oh, great,' Mhatre said.

'He also told me that this has to be the last time you step out of line. And he means it.'

Mhatre nodded. He knew Khan meant it.

'Must have been some day for you, huh? With the anniversary and all?'

Mhatre made a face but said nothing.

They drank in silence for a while. Patankar took it slow. Mhatre's sips soon turned into swigs.

'The woman,' Patankar said, finally.

'What?' Mhatre asked.

'Just go with this. There was a woman with Bhatia when they met Singh, and there was a woman with Bhatia when they checked into that hotel. Is it safe to assume that they're the same woman?'

Mhatre nodded without hesitation.

'Convince me,' Patankar said.

Mhatre's tongue was starting to feel just a little heavy but his brain was still working. His mentor-cum-friend liked to give him exercises like these.

'Well, firstly, if it isn't the same woman, it means Bhatia had brought *two* women on board. And that isn't like Bhatia. If he was coming out of retirement, it has to be a special job and he'd want minimum people in the know. Singh for his smuggling network, Ansari because he's, well, multi-purpose, and the woman for whatever role she's playing.'

Patankar nodded in approval.

'You know,' Patankar finally said, 'I can't help thinking if we've been approaching this from the wrong angle.'

'As in?' Mhatre asked.

'As in, we've been so taken up with Bhatia from the start because he was a key player when it came to the Shivaji Park attack. But this woman—whoever she is—Singh says he was scared of her.'

'What are you saying?'

'If Bhatia was such a key player in this particular job, why are the woman and Ansari still meeting each other now that he's dead?'

Mhatre, who had just raised his glass to his lips, put it down.

'Could that be why Bhatia was killed?' he wondered aloud. 'Because he had served his purpose for the woman?'

Both cops looked at each other, both thinking the same thing.

Who the hell is this woman?

27

Bhatia watched her silently as she slipped the backpack off her shoulders and laid it on the floor. She, as usual, hardly spoke.

Quickly, she removed the clothes from inside the backpack and placed them aside before prying open the false bottom. She pulled out the two pistols hidden there and handed them to him.

He examined the guns for a moment before placing them on the table. Silently, she passed on the box of 9 mm rounds. Then she went over to the bed and sat down.

'No trouble on the way, I hope?' Bhatia asked.

She just shook her head.

They were in a hotel room in Mussoorie, where a client was supposed to take delivery of the arsenal in six hours.

After his run-in with the police following the Shivaji Park incident, Bhatia had spent three days at a hotel at Marine Drive and made sure he wasn't being watched, before finally going to the Lokhandwala Complex.

His aide, Jafar, had told him that the girl seemed to be doing okay. She spoke very little but was eating well and didn't seem to be ill. At Bhatia's instructions, Jafar had got her a laptop and installed an internet router in the house. Four days later, Jafar had let himself in with his key to find her doing push-ups on the floor, with an instructional video playing on the laptop. She had been working out regularly since then, doing body-building exercises.

By the time Bhatia returned, almost six weeks after he'd left her there, she no longer looked fragile and delicate. The muscles were well defined, there was a hardness to her appearance and she seemed more confident.

'She still won't go out, though,' Jafar told Bhatia.

All three of them left for Punjab that same night. The incident at Shivaji Park had changed things for Bhatia. It had brought a lot of heat down on him, and Mumbai was no longer safe for him. The money he had made, though, would see him through nicely for a long time, and there were plenty of opportunities to be explored in other places.

'Let me work for you,' she had said to him after they reached his hometown.

'Do you know what I do?' he asked.

'I have a fair idea. And I need to repay you somehow.'

Bhatia had been prepared to turn her down, but he knew that there was nowhere she could survive on her own without inviting – or dispensing – violence. There was a world of people out there that would jump at the chance of taking advantage of a young girl on her own. She had already tasted blood twice – she wouldn't hesitate to bathe in it if the necessity presented itself again. Apart from the fact that he didn't want her troubles leading back to him, he recognised the use he could put her to.

Her training had been short and simple. How to spot a tail. How to lose one. Basic self-defence.

Only then did he tell her what he precisely did for a living. He had a contact in the ordnance factory in Nagpur who helped him get sophisticated arms. Nothing that would attract too much attention. A couple of pistols here, a grenade there. Orders for such weaponry were few and far between, with most criminal elements being happy using country-made firearms made in north India. But there were still those who required a weapon of good quality every now and then, mostly to show off, and weapons licences came with strict checks and rules. Thus, he had a regular clientele who preferred to dispense with such formalities.

The Shivaji Park incident was the first time anyone had asked for a fragmentation grenade, and even his contact in the ordnance factory had been surprised. But the pay-off was huge, and he was able to buy so many layers in the delivery that the police had been unable to establish any concrete link to him.

Chhaya, with her diminutive frame and a natural aversion to human contact which made her instinctively avoid attention, turned out to be the perfect courier. He taught her how she could use her looks to her advantage, and over the years, she learned how to act as if she actually cared about the person she was using as a means to an end.

She had discovered her sexuality only by accident, while using another girl for a job while smuggling a factory-made revolver from Nagpur to Hampi. She spent two days with the girl, during which they toured Hampi in the day and made tender love at night, the girl making her discover new things about her own body.

Chhaya, a name that Bhatia eventually gave her because he had to call her something, disappeared without a trace on the third day, leaving the girl wondering what happened for a long time.

She knew she would do the same to Sanika as well. Which wouldn't be a problem because she had no plans of returning to the city anyway. It was in this city that she first discovered how ugly humanity really was, and it was here that she first took a life. With the money she had received for the job — the money that Bhatia had received, actually — she could disappear forever.

Bhatia had signed his own death warrant without even knowing it. He was fated to die soon enough anyway. The fire at Sitaara Hotel had just sped up the process, as it gave her the perfect opportunity to pass it off as an accident.

They had both been catching a nap, as they had to pick up the delivery together later that night. With the amount of money involved, Bhatia wasn't taking any chances. The heat from the fire woke her up first and Bhatia a second later.

'Grab everything,' he'd hissed at her. 'We can't leave any traces.'

He went to the bathroom to get his clothes. As he came out, she punched him in the throat. He dropped his clothes as both his hands went to his throat, and she grabbed him by the hair and shoved him backwards, slamming his head against the metal doorknob.

Quickly, she ran to the staircase landing, where she had noticed gas cutters on her way up when they had checked in. She had made a trip to the third floor out of curiosity and seen workers with more gas cutters working on the renovation. She was willing to bet that one of the cutters was responsible for the fire. The ones on the lower landing seemed to be there as backup.

She grabbed one and was running back to the room when she came face to face with the manager. No doubt, he was going about evacuating the floor. Without pausing to think, she grabbed him by the throat and depressed his jugular vein, letting him fall to the ground. He had seen her face and she couldn't take a chance.

Running to the room, she grabbed the sheet off the bed and laid it over the unconscious Bhatia. Then she pressed the lever of the cutter, held a lighted match to the jet of gas that emerged and set it on fire. Next, she went to the bathroom and grabbed all the towels, as well as the remaining sheets on the bed, before running out. She laid the bundle of linen out at the top of the staircase and went to the room one last time. The sheet on Bhatia's body was in flames and she could smell burning flesh as well.

She grabbed only her burqa and purse, which contained money, her cellphone and their forged identity documents. She stepped over the towels and bedsheets at the staircase and then lit them afire as well. Within seconds, the flames *started shooting upwards. She threw the gas cutter into the flames.*

Putting on the burqa, she sped downstairs and paused at the reception desk only long enough to get the photocopies of their documents from the drawer, before exiting the hotel to slip into the crowd outside. People reached out to help her but she waved them off.

She fled to an adjacent street and hailed a taxi to Bandra. On the way, she destroyed the SIM card in her phone and slipped in a new one.

The doorbell to Sanika's apartment rang and she came back to the present. Soundlessly, she went to the door to see a deliveryman with a medium-size parcel in his hands.

'Jolene Alva?' he asked. She nodded.

Niyaz Ansari handed her the parcel, turned and walked away, not knowing that the woman in the burqa who had given him the address was the same as the one receiving the parcel from him.

28

Oscar walked into the noisy bar and looked around for a place to sit. His work for the day had ended earlier than he had expected it to, and he had wanted to come here for old times' sake.

He remembered it from his old days in the police force. Tucked away in a corner of one of the side lanes of one of the many lanes branching out from Metro Cinema, the bar had a forbidding exterior which prevented most people from entering it. Close by, another bar, which was a little more affordable, was buzzing with patrons of all ages and genders. It looked more inviting and a first-timer would automatically gravitate to that one.

This joint, on the other hand, looked like a dance bar, with a closed-off glass door and, at the entrance, there was a mean-looking guard who was actually very friendly. It did have a tiny live band in one area, but also a section further inside which was closed off. It was a haven for those who liked to drink alone.

Intersections

Oscar entered the inner section and looked around as the door swung shut behind him. All the tables were occupied, and the only available seat was in front of another man who was drinking by himself.

Oscar approached warily, not knowing whether the young, burly man was a peaceable drinker or the aggressive kind. The man noticed him and seemed to understand. He waved his right hand slightly, indicating that he was fine sharing tables, and Oscar gratefully took the seat in front of him.

He waited to place his order before he spoke.

'By any chance,' he said, 'are you API Uday Mhatre? Or is it PI now?'

Mhatre sighed. This was one result of his fame that he definitely did not enjoy.

'What gave me away?' he asked with a crooked smile.

Oscar gave a light laugh.

'You're a legend even to us former cops, you know.'

Mhatre looked at Oscar with interest.

'Really ... sir?' he said, adding the last part in deference to Oscar's obvious seniority in terms of age.

'I'm going out on a limb here, Mr Mhatre,' Oscar said, 'and suggesting that you might, just *might*, have heard my name. Oscar Fernandes.'

Mhatre sat up.

'*Arrey bhen* ... I mean, wow. Indeed I have, sir.'

The cop inside Mhatre took over on autopilot. The

word 'sir' would automatically attach itself at the end of every sentence from here on.

'"Oscar", please,' the older man said as they shook hands warmly. Then they clinked glasses and sipped their drinks.

'What brings you to the city, sir?' Mhatre asked. Oscar's plea notwithstanding, Mhatre's training would never let him address the older man by name.

'Oh, lending a friend a hand. A little freelance investigation, if you will.'

'Anything I can help with, sir? The case I'm working on has reached a stalemate. I spent all of today just sitting idle in the office.'

Oscar waved aside the offer. 'I'm willing to bet it's going to turn out to be nothing. But it's for a friend, so …'

Mhatre got the hint and changed the subject.

'You might know my reporting head, sir. PI Sharad Patankar?'

Oscar took a sip before he answered.

'Is the bastard still murdering Hindi songs?'

'He's already butchered many of my favourites, and I don't see him stopping anytime soon. You worked with him, sir?'

Oscar shook his head. 'Never got that chance, but we're batchmates. Even back in the MPA, he had all the makings of a good leader.'

'No wonder he's heading the squad now.'

Intersections

Mhatre brought Oscar up to speed with the genesis of the Zone I squad, and Oscar seemed genuinely impressed by the idea. Conversation, inevitably, veered to the Shivaji Park incident and the liquor flowed freely as the conversation got serious.

The bar had started emptying when Oscar lit a cigarette and leaned back in his seat.

'You seem to understand pain, Uday,' he said.

Mhatre paused in the middle of a sip. 'Well, sir, it seems so do you. I mean, only someone who understands pain can identify someone else who does, right?'

Oscar took a long swig and sighed. 'How much do you know about my last case?' he asked.

Mhatre told him.

During Oscar's last month on the job, Ankit Tripathi, barely eighteen years old, had broken into the house of an elderly couple staying by themselves in Borivali, stabbed them both to death and robbed the house. An hour later, a Crime Branch officer having tea at a roadside stall happened to notice Ankit as he was walking back to his own house, a duffel bag full of his spoils in hand. The officer became suspicious because Ankit's shirt was very obviously flecked with bloodstains. The cop caught hold of Ankit, and Ankit tried to attack him with the same meat cleaver he had used on the old couple. The officer took two slashes on his arm before whipping out his service pistol, turning it around and hitting Ankit on the head with the butt, knocking him out.

The case landed in Oscar's lap, who was at the time with the Borivali Police Station. The accused was already under arrest, caught with the proceeds of his crime, and with the murder weapon on his person. It was an open-and-shut case.

Which is why no one understood why Oscar put in his papers the same day that he filed the chargesheet against Ankit in the court. His resignation letter only cited 'personal reasons', and the commissioner of police called him in for a personal meeting. No one knew what happened in that meeting, but when Oscar walked out an hour later, his resignation had been accepted. He left the city the same day and never returned—except once, to depose as a witness in the case.

Mhatre recounted all of this to Oscar, who just sat back listening, his eyes in the shadows.

'That wasn't Ankit's first offence,' he finally said in a low voice.

Mhatre leaned forward. 'Really?' he asked.

Oscar took two slow drags of his cigarette before he spoke again. 'He was a few months shy of eighteen when I first detained him for attempted robbery.'

'Wait, what?' Mhatre asked, abruptly alert. The whiskey had started to take effect but he felt his instincts sharpen.

Oscar gave a wry smile before he went on. In the larger scheme of things, as defined by the Mumbai Police, Ankit's first offence hardly made a dent.

'He tried to rob a jeweller who was on his way home after shutting shop for the day. He had somehow got his hands on a meat cleaver, and had used it to try and scare the jeweller into giving up his day's earnings. The jeweller, who was several kilogrammes heavier and at least a foot taller, had slapped the meat cleaver out of Ankit's hand, given him the bashing of his life, and dragged him to the Borivali Police Station — where I was posted at the time. I was on night duty then.'

Mhatre sensed that the story was about to get darker.

'What happened after that?' he asked.

'His father literally fell at my feet and begged me to give him another chance, saying his life would be ruined in juvenile detention. He was technically a minor, right? Even the jeweller took pity on the boy, who had turned to crime because his garage mechanic father could not provide him with the luxuries he wanted. My fucker of a senior PI said it was not worth it if the jeweller himself did not want to register a complaint.'

'You had to let him go,' Mhatre guessed.

'Against every bloody instinct, I had to let him go. And three months later, he killed the elderly couple before robbing their house.'

'*Madarchod* …' Mhatre breathed.

Oscar took another long swig of his drink.

'And now, I have to live with the fact that, had I put in a little more effort and convinced that jeweller to file an FIR, that poor helpless couple would have been alive today.'

Mhatre thought of the five names burned into his own brain.

Shireen, Reema, Sehar, Vasant and Ashok.

29

Rohit walked out of the classroom fighting the urge to shout for joy.

The exams were finally over. He would be meeting Rupa in the evening at their favourite spot on the beach, and they would plan their weekend getaway. And then, for two blissful days ...

Rohit smiled dreamily, and in the process almost bumped into a passing teacher.

'Careful, child,' the chubby-faced Mr Krishnamoorthy said mildly.

Rohit mumbled an apology and Mr Krishnamoorthy waved it off. 'Here, have some cake,' he said, offering a piece from a paper plate he was carrying.

Startled, Rohit accepted the piece that his teacher held out. Not knowing what else to say, he blurted, 'It's ... your birthday, sir?'

'Haha. No, young man. Ms Rupa is getting engaged tomorrow. We're having a little party in the staffroom.'

Rohit felt the ground slip from beneath his feet.

'Ms ... Ms Rupa ...?' he stammered.

'I think she teaches your class English, doesn't she?'

Rohit could only nod.

Mr Krishnamoorthy leaned forward conspiratorially. 'Don't tell anyone, eh? She'll announce it formally in class next week,' he said, before winking at him and striding off.

In a daze, Rohit walked to the gate, not even realising when the piece of cake crumbled from his hand into a creamy mess at his feet. Every fibre of his being wanted to barge into the staffroom and demand an explanation from Rupa. With superhuman effort, he restrained himself, mounted his bicycle and pedalled away.

Not now, he thought. *Not now. Decisions made in anger are almost always the wrong ones.*

Rupa had told him that once.

It had been hours since he had got to the beach and there was no sign of Rupa.

Why, he kept thinking. *How could she do this to me?*

Slowly, as the news sunk in, his mind started building theories.

Was it something he had done? Impossible. Things were beautiful between them the last time they had met.

What, then, could it be?

Had she just been leading him on? But why? Out of malice? Again, impossible. Out of pity? No. It had felt

Intersections

real. It was the purest thing he had experienced, and there was no way it could be fake.

It was during the second hour of his waiting that an explanation occurred to him.

Parental pressure. Yes. That had to be it. Her parents must have found a groom for her. And how was she going to tell them that she loved someone twelve years younger than herself? A student of hers, at that.

The more he thought about it, the more he was convinced of his theory.

Another half an hour passed before he finally accepted that she was not coming. By the time he returned to his bicycle, he knew that he had to do something.

He cycled hard and made it back to his college just in time. He parked his bicycle and waited till he saw Mr Krishnamoorthy walking towards the gate. Then he entered, trying to look as casual as he could.

He pretended to look up and suddenly spot him, and stopped in his tracks. Mr Krishnamoorthy saw him too and smiled.

'I just ... I never said thank you. For the cake,' Rohit said, feeling foolish. Mr Krishnamoorthy grinned.

'Don't mention it, young man. Don't mention it.'

'I must also convey my best wishes to Ms Rupa. She has always been nice to me. You know, sir, when my mother passed away, she sought me out and told me I could talk to her. It was really kind of her.'

Mr Krishnamoorthy's genial face clouded over.

'Ah, yes. I heard about that, child. I can't imagine what you must have gone through. But yes, Ms Rupa is a gem of a person.'

'True, sir,' Rohit said earnestly.

'Tell you what,' Mr Krishnamoorthy said. 'I'm going to her engagement ceremony tomorrow evening. I'll make sure to convey your wishes.'

Rohit smiled. 'Thank you, sir,' he said earnestly. 'Thank you so much.'

30

Mhatre was at Sitaara Hotel. It was deserted, its walls charred. All around the lobby, there were bits and pieces of partly burned furniture. Shards of glass crunched under his shoes as he tramped through the ruined premises.

He had no idea why he was here, or when he got here. Blackouts were becoming a regular feature due to his heavy drinking habit, but he had never ended up anywhere apart from his house in Girgaum after a bout of boozing.

He crossed the lobby and went up to the first floor, where Bhatia and the woman had been staying as Afzal and Fatima Siddiqui. The rooms had open doors through which the emptiness inside was clearly visible.

Except for the last one. The door was not locked but slightly ajar, not wide open like the others. He stood outside the room for a long time before reaching out and pushing the door, which opened further, the sound echoing in the silence.

He did not want to enter. And he wanted to enter as well. He fought with himself for a while before he finally stepped inside.

They were sprawled out on the floor in the semi-darkness. He moved closer for a better look, even though he somehow already knew who they were.

Shireen, Reema, Sehar, Vasant and Ashok. They were lying from left to right in exactly the order that their names always repeated themselves in his head. He willed himself to look away but couldn't. Instead, he found himself going down on one knee. His brain screamed at him to stop but his hand reached out to touch little Sehar's blood-soaked form.

Mhatre woke up with a stifled cry and nearly fell off his bed.

It took a minute for his breathing to return to normal, by which time he slowly realised that he was in his own house. He stood up and looked out the window. It was early evening.

That morning, he had texted Patankar, asking if he could take the day off. The last few days had been taxing, especially emotionally, and he had decided he needed the rest. Patankar replied with a yes, and added a line on how he should not be drinking so much.

Next, Mhatre had texted Oscar, telling him it had been nice to run into him the previous night. Oscar texted back saying he hoped Mhatre was okay, as he had got quite drunk, and that they should catch up before he left the city. Mhatre agreed with alacrity.

He had gone through the motions of having tea and breakfast before returning to bed, not knowing what else to do. The conversation with Oscar kept playing itself in his head and he didn't realise when he had fallen asleep again. Only for the nightmare to wake him up.

Mhatre turned around from the window. The headache was not as intense as it had been in the morning, but it was still there. He drank some water and quickly got dressed, slipping his gun into the back of his waistband and letting his shirt fall over it.

He passed a couple of his neighbours on his way out but no one nodded to or greeted him. He was unpopular, and he was hardly surprised at that. Apart from his, most of the apartments were occupied by cops with families. It was only because of the political backing that he enjoyed that he had got entire quarters to himself in the first place. And then there was the matter of his coming home drunk night after night.

Mhatre got on his motorbike, which his father had presented him when he became a police officer. He had tried to get his parents to move to Mumbai with him when he got his posting, but they were happy in their sleepy little village near Nashik. Sometimes he wondered how he'd have turned out had they stayed together.

Mhatre knew where he was going and got there quickly. The street in Madanpura was humming with activity and he had trouble finding a parking spot, although he got one eventually. He made the rest of the way to the building on foot. Crossing the street, he sat down at the bus stop, watching the building and waiting for his prey.

He did not have to wait for long before Niyaz Ansari came out of the gate, all dressed up as if he was going to attend a social function. He seemed to be in a good mood as he waved and exchanged greetings with people on his way to his bike.

Mhatre was thinking about Ankit Tripathi and his two aged victims as he stood up and began to cross back to the building. Then he thought about the others.

Shireen, Reema, Sehar, Vasant and Ashok.

Just as Ansari laid a hand on the handlebar of his bike, Mhatre came up from behind and wrapped an arm firmly around his shoulder. Ansari turned to see who it was and his face changed into a mask of terror.

'I'm armed,' Mhatre said quietly. 'And I'm in a very bad mood. If you come with me without causing any trouble, you will not be harmed. That's a promise.'

Ansari went numb, but only briefly. Without warning, he pushed Mhatre away from him violently. Mhatre, who had not been expecting this, lost his balance and fell on a parked motorbike behind him. The vehicle crashed into the one behind it and the domino effect brought the entire row of bikes down.

Swearing, Mhatre stood up, not stopping to check if he was hurt, and started in the direction he had seen Ansari go when he fell. Both men ran madly through the crowds, which were impeding their progress.

Ansari was lighter and faster, but Mhatre was driven by the fury inside him as he pelted on, drawing closer and closer to Ansari. Ansari did not even look back once. All of his efforts were focused on just getting away.

He failed to notice a wooden cart laden with fast food that a vendor was pushing out of a side lane, and it crashed into him, sending him to the ground hard. He managed to save his face, letting his hands take the impact instead.

The next instant, Mhatre pounced on him and pulled him to his feet, struggling and flailing.

People, hurrying for their own reasons through the crowded street, started slowing down to watch, and slowly formed a circle around the two men as they scuffled.

'What are you doing?' a man called out.

'Let him go!' another said.

'Help!' Ansari shouted. 'Help me! He's a murderer!'

'Shut up, you bastard!' Mhatre said, his teeth bared in rage, and pulled his gun out while holding Ansari in a stranglehold with the free arm.

The crowd started panicking as Mhatre brought up the gun and rammed it against Ansari's temple.

'He'll kill the poor man!' a woman screamed.

'Police!' Mhatre shouted. 'I'm a cop! This man is a suspect!'

Ansari stepped hard on Mhatre's foot, causing his grip to loosen. Mhatre yelled in pain and Ansari swiftly took to his heels.

Mhatre tried to go after him but found his path blocked by a hostile crowd.

'Is this how you cops do things now?' an old man shouted.

'What is this? Is this a police state?'

'You think you can do anything to us poor people because you have a smart uniform to wear?'

'Call the media. Tell them how this policeman behaved!'

Mhatre roared with frustration as Ansari disappeared into the crowd.

31

One of the reasons Patankar was always seen tapping away at his phone was because he preferred text messages over calls. Another reason was that he liked to trawl social media for anything that might warrant a closer look.

A surprisingly large number of people liked to post unverified posts and videos, accompanied by the wildest of allegations, on their social media accounts, simply to grab some eyeballs. To Patankar's surprise, such people had hundreds of followers who blindly shared these on their own accounts without questions. The online version of mob mentality.

He still remembered how one such message had sparked off communal tension in the Mahim area around seven years ago, because someone had circulated a picture of a dead body on WhatsApp, claiming that he had died in the Mahim Police Station lock-up after being tortured by the police simply because of his religion.

Heavy patrolling and deployment had been enforced in the entire Mahim area for two days while Patankar, who was with the Crime Branch at the time, scoured all the morgues in the city till he found the dead body in the picture. It was the corpse of a victim of a road accident who had died in Borivali the same morning that the message had been circulated.

While a lot of people tended to ignore forwarded messages or media files, Patankar always made it a point to take a look before dismissing them.

That evening, Patankar was scrolling through his messages when he got a fresh one. It was a link to a Facebook post of someone he didn't know, but the link was forwarded to him by a friend. He opened the post and went through it.

'SEE HOW THIS POLICE ARE HARASSING INNOCENCE PEOPLES EVERY DAY IN MALEGAON FOR NO REASONS THIS IS WHAT IS DEMOCRACY WE ARE LIVING!!!!'

The atrociously worded caption was accompanied by a video, where a man was holding another with his forearm around his throat and had a gun to his head with the other hand.

Only, the location was not Malegaon; the man being assaulted was Niyaz Ansari and the man with the gun was API Uday Mhatre.

'Kadam!' Patankar yelled, looking at the 'likes' and 'shares' the post was getting. 'Call that friend of yours in Cyber right now! We need to get a post taken off Facebook.'

He forwarded the link to Kadam and Khan, and then called Khan immediately. Khan didn't answer. Patankar called again. Khan's orderly answered.

'Khan sir is in a meeting with Joint CP sir …' he began.

'Listen to me very carefully. Go to Joint CP sir's orderly, tell him it is an emergency and get Khan sir's phone to him right now. I don't want to call Joint CP sir directly, but I will if I have to and then I'll have to tell him how I had to go up the chain of command because you didn't cooperate with me.' Patankar spoke each word slowly and deliberately.

In about thirty seconds, Khan was on the line.

'Really sorry, sir,' Patankar said. 'But I've just sent you something on WhatsApp and it is very, very urgent. I'm leaving right now and will wait for you at your office.'

'Okay, Patankar,' a puzzled Khan said.

Patankar stood up and rushed to the door, passing a stupefied Kadam, who was watching the video on her own cellphone. She looked up at him, her mouth open in shock, but he didn't stop to explain.

As he got into the police SUV and sped to Khan's office, he dialled Mhatre's number. When the call was answered, he said, 'I don't know where you are, and I don't care, but get to Khan's office without delay.'

Patankar hung up before Mhatre could say anything and did not look at his phone again till he pulled up outside Khan's office. The constable on the ground floor told him Khan wasn't there yet, so he paced around outside, hoping Mhatre would show up before Khan did.

He called Kadam and asked her what the status was, and she told him that the Cyber Cell was working on it.

'Ask them to work faster!' he snapped and hung up.

It was sheer misfortune that Khan had been at the joint commissioner's office when he had called him up, Patankar thought. Now Khan would be duty-bound to share the matter with the joint CP, who would, without question, tell the commissioner as well. It was completely out of Khan's hands, even if he had wanted to shield Mhatre somehow, which Patankar didn't think was possible in the first place.

Mhatre's bike came to a stop outside the office and he dashed up to Patankar. One look at his superior's face told Mhatre what was wrong.

'How?' he asked, looking away.

'Someone shot a video and put it up on Facebook.'

Mhatre swore. 'I suppose saying I'm sorry won't matter?' he asked.

'Are you?' Patankar said, deathly calm. 'Are you, really?'

Mhatre looked away again.

'You know, Uday,' Patankar said, stepping closer. 'All of us who were even remotely connected to the Shivaji Park case were affected by it. No one walks away from something like that without scars. I personally recorded statements from the family of all those who died that day. But you don't see any of us giving ourselves the licence to behave in the manner you have these past few days.'

'It's not like that, sir,' Mhatre said.

'Then what is it like, Uday? Tell me what it is like, because I'd really like to figure this out, if only for my own satisfaction. I have to be literally the only person who stands by you every fucking time, and the more I do that, the more out-of-hand you get.'

Mhatre turned away and brought out his pack of cigarettes. Patankar caught hold of his shoulder and turned him back around to face him.

'Come on, tell me,' Patankar said, bringing his face close to Mhatre's. 'What's the big secret? What's this deep, dark reason why you keep abusing the trust of all those around you all the time?'

Mhatre's mouth went tight and his eyes were as narrow as slits.

'Fine,' he spat. 'You really want to know, sir?'

Patankar said nothing.

Mhatre took a deep breath.

'Will you two at least take it off the street before someone shoots another video?'

Khan's growl made them both spin around. Mhatre stepped away and looked down.

'Sorry, sir,' Patankar said. 'After you, sir.'

Mhatre stepped up to the entrance.

'Oh, you don't need to come,' Khan said to Mhatre. He held out an envelope.

'That's your suspension order. Signed by the CP ten minutes ago.'

32

Kadam was running out of methods, but at least she had some results.

The CDRs of the number that Ansari had dialled before his SIM card went inactive had only confirmed what she already suspected, that the number was used by the elusive woman in the burqa. The number had become active mere minutes after the Sitaara hotel fire, and had gone out of service the same day as Ansari's old number.

The last location of the woman's number was in Bandra West, and the area had three hotels where she could have been staying. Kadam decided to check them out, hoping the woman wasn't staying with someone. While Patankar was speeding to Khan's office, Kadam coordinated with the Cyber Cell to have the post taken off Facebook, while simultaneously entering the names of all the three hotels in separate tabs on her browser.

As she waited for a response from the Cyber Cell, she began calling up the hotels. Her step was based on a simple assumption. With Bhatia dead, the woman would be less likely to use the burqa as much as she had in the past. A woman in a burqa checking into a hotel alone was unheard of. There was nothing officially wrong with it per se, but in India, that simply did not happen. She wasn't sure if the hotels would even let such a woman stay, unless she was accompanied by another, similarly attired.

Which meant she either had another accomplice, maybe Ansari, who helped her on this front, or she had had to discard the burqa and show her face. She would definitely change her appearance once she left the city. Maybe a haircut, maybe a new hair colour.

Kadam hit the jackpot at the second hotel she called. A young woman had stayed there for two days before checking out abruptly. The day she checked out was the day the woman's number went inactive. Kadam asked the hotel authorities to send all the woman's details to her immediately. The manager said he'd have to bring the owner into the loop, but it was a mere formality.

'If I don't have the details in my inbox in the next one hour,' she told the manager, 'I'll come down to the hotel myself. I don't think your guests need to see a cop marching in, so I'd suggest you deliver pronto.'

With no other leads, she turned to her laptop again and sent out an email to all major cellular service-providers, seeking information on all numbers that had travelled from Bandra Bandstand to the Mahim Dargah on the day that Ansari met the woman. She restricted the time frame to between the time the woman had departed from Bandstand to three hours later, allowing for a margin of error. If the woman had stayed in the dargah beyond that time period, she'd have to go for a longer time frame.

It could add up to thousands of numbers, and she was going to have to ask Patankar to get some constables to help her. None of them was going to be happy.

The police call it 'dump data analysis' and it is arguably one of the most tedious tasks of an investigation. Cops only turn to it as a last resort—and for good reason. It involves analysing the registration details of thousands of numbers that have passed through a particular location at the given time, and eliminating each one till the list trickles down to a few suspects. Then, a new analysis of those numbers begins. It can drive the most patient cops up the wall.

She was fervently praying that it didn't come to that, when she received a message from the Cyber Cell informing her that Facebook had agreed to take the post down. She sighed with relief just as Patankar walked in, looking completely dejected.

She followed him into his cabin and they both sat down.

'How bad?' she asked.

'He's suspended. Khan didn't even want to transfer him to Local Arms. Just sent him packing the minute he saw him.'

Local Arms was a supplementary force, where cops who ran afoul of their seniors were transferred. It was a punishment posting, where duties involved standing long hours in the sun or rain, enforcing security for events like visits of political leaders or celebrity events.

Kadam grimaced. 'What happens now?'

'The usual. Departmental Enquiry. Action. The CP is pretty angry. Pretty sure some politician or another will step in at some point, and if he's lucky, Uday will get off with a negative remark in his ACR after serving a long period of suspension.'

ACRs, annual confidential reports, are made every year, where a policeman's performance for the year is reviewed. This helps his superiors decide his next promotion or posting, or eligibility for that year's medals for good service. Mhatre had one for the Shivaji Park incident. Patankar had earned two in his career, and while Kadam hadn't received one yet, her track record so far indicated that she would get at least one for exemplary service further into her career.

'Has the post been taken off?' Patankar asked.

'Yes, sir.'

'Where are we on the Bandra connection?'

'Oh, let me check,' Kadam said, looking at her watch. The deadline she had given to the hotel manager was approaching.

She went to her laptop and, sure enough, the manager had emailed her the details. She took a printout and returned to Patankar's office. Briefly, she told him what steps she had taken, and placed the printout on his desk.

'Tanushree Sachdeva,' Patankar read, picking it up. Kadam moved around his desk to stand behind him so that she could read it at the same time.

The supposed Tanushree Sachdeva had checked in two days earlier for a period of five days, but had checked out prematurely, citing a personal emergency. She had submitted an Aadhaar card, but that was easy to forge. Her place of residence was stated to be New Delhi and Patankar was sure the address was a bogus one.

But, for the first time, they had a face to work with.

The hotel manager had taken a picture of her, using a small camera mounted on the monitor of his computer, facing away from him. It was usual practice at hotels. Long hair left loose, small face, average features and a tiny mole on her left cheek, close to the chin. Both cops were willing to bet that the mole was nothing but make-up. She was wearing a red bindi and large round earrings.

'Finally, some good news,' Patankar said.

Kadam nodded, silently hoping this lead would pan out enough to save her the trouble of going through the dump data. It wasn't just about the tedium. This woman had already been in the city for nearly a week, which meant that whatever her mission was, it could be executed any day.

'Circulate it, for what it's worth,' Patankar told her. 'I'll do the same. Get down to the hotel tomorrow and get CCTV footage for the time that she was there. We'll see what else comes up.'

'Yes, sir,' Kadam said. She moved towards the door but stopped midway.

'Sir,' she said.

Patankar, who had just picked up his phone, looked at her enquiringly.

'Uday ... is he okay?'

'Frankly, Sushmita,' Patankar said, 'I don't really care—right now.'

33

It was almost evening. Rohit waited patiently near a bus stop some distance away from his college. It was the route that Mr Krishnamoorthy took to drive from the college to his house.

Now, as Mr Krishnamoorthy's car pulled out of the campus, Rohit swung himself onto his bicycle and started following him. He took care to maintain his distance and followed him undetected all the way to his house in Dadar.

After another wait, Mr Krishnamoorthy emerged from the building with his wife, both decked up for the celebrations. They got into his car and Rohit once again fell into place behind them. Patiently, he pedalled after the car till it stopped outside the hall in Tardeo rented for the occasion.

He let Mr Krishnamoorthy and his wife enter the hall before he pulled up across the street from it. The board at the entrance announced the engagement ceremony of 'Anuj & Rupa' on the first floor.

He smiled. He had a name.

Putting on his best lost expression, he went up to the hall on the first floor. He was dressed in a formal shirt and trousers. His father had looked curiously at him as he left, but he hadn't said anything, and Rohit didn't feel the need to explain his attire.

In the hall, everyone was engaged in conversation with someone or the other. He removed his phone from his pocket and stuck it to his ear. Pretending to be in conversation with someone, he started moving through the crowd, trying to catch what they were saying.

It took time, but he eventually overheard someone say on his own phone, 'It's Anuj's engagement … Yes, our Anuj Sodhi … Yeah, man. It was quite sudden. Apparently they met a week ago and hit it off like nobody's business … Of course, there's still time till the wedding …'

Rohit moved away, keeping an eye on Mr Krishnamoorthy, who was at the other end of the hall. He went as close to the dais as he safely could, just in time to see the would-be-groom climb up on it. The entire hall erupted in cheers, and Rohit slipped out.

Exiting the compound, he searched for, and found, a small Chinese food joint, where he ordered a fried rice. Then he opened Facebook and went through the profiles of all the men named Anuj Sodhi till he found the right one. He carefully checked all the profile pictures to make sure it was the same man he had seen in the hall.

Then he waited.

Like a beast of prey, he thought.

It was almost midnight by the time Anuj and his parents left the hall. Anuj was practically glowing, and so were his parents, as they got into a cab to go to their hotel.

'I'm really happy you agreed to the engagement at such short notice,' his father was saying. 'It's just a ceremony, you know. Sort of meant to finalise things. You both take your time. The wedding can happen whenever you want it to.'

Anuj only nodded. When he had told his father that he liked Rupa, his father had insisted on an immediate engagement. Anuj himself thought it was too rushed, and so did Rupa, but both their parents had been insistent, and ultimately, the young couple gave in. Besides, they admitted, they *did* like each other a lot.

They met for the first time the day he reached Mumbai, and met almost every day after that. Rupa, a lecturer with a junior college in Mumbai, made sure she could meet him despite the fact that mid-term exams were underway at her college. Anuj had told his boss in Aurangabad that he would have to work from Mumbai till things finalised. Fortunately, his boss had agreed.

'Just bloody go on leave, man,' his boss had told him jovially. 'If a compulsive workaholic like you has finally found his potential life-partner, I wouldn't dare interfere with destiny. Forget work for a while.'

Anuj smiled to himself, reflecting that he loved his job as a lawyer too much to stay away from it unnecessarily. He was the kind that worked most weekends.

Anuj was still smiling as the cab reached the hotel in Mumbai Central. He told his parents to go on to their room while he paid the driver. Just as the cab drove off, he heard someone call his name.

'Mr Sodhi?' the teenage boy asked. 'Mr Anuj Sodhi?'

Anuj looked up at the stranger. 'I'm sorry, do I know you?'

The boy grinned. 'I'm Ms Rupa's student,' he said. 'Some of us were planning something for her ... you know, like, a surprise ... to congratulate her on her engagement. I was kind of hoping we could rope you in.'

Anuj smiled. 'Sure,' he said. 'What can I do?'

In his mind, Rohit was thinking how lucky he was that Anuj had sent his parents up to their room. Now Anuj would be the only one who had seen his face, and soon that wouldn't be an issue anyway.

'Well,' he said, stepping closer. 'I have a plan.'

Rohit's hand went to his back.

At that instant, Oscar Fernandes stepped out of the shadows and wrapped one burly forearm around Rohit's throat.

'What the hell!' Anuj said, as Rohit struggled in Oscar's grip.

'Congratulations on the engagement, Anuj,' Oscar said, as, with his other hand, he wrested Rohit's hand from behind him and brought it to the front, revealing the large kitchen knife he was holding.

Anuj froze.

'What ... what's happening, Mr ... Mr ...' he stuttered, remembering the encounter with Oscar but not his name.

'It's Fernandes,' Oscar said, forcing a struggling Rohit face-down on the ground. 'Oscar Fernandes. From nowhere in particular.'

Rohit continued to struggle and shout as Oscar fought to hold both his hands behind him.

'Calm down, boy,' Oscar growled and managed to wrest the knife out of his hand and throw it a distance away.

'Pick that up, Anuj!' Oscar called, pinning Rohit to the ground.

'*No!*' Rohit yelled. '*Let me go!*'

'I'll ... I'll call the cops ...' Anuj stammered as his parents and the hotel staff ran over to check what was happening.

Oscar made a face just as a car came roaring up to them.

'Give me a little more credit!' Oscar said to Anuj, as the door to the car opened and Patankar jumped out, gun drawn.

'What the hell, Oscar?' Patankar said, keeping his gun trained on the still struggling boy.

'Handcuffs, Sharad. We need handcuffs here, not guns.'

34

A week earlier, Deepak, Rohit's father, had called Oscar and requested a favour. Deepak ran a travel agency on D.N. Road and had got to know Oscar when the latter was posted with the local police station. After noticing that Rohit's absences in the evening were getting more and more frequent, and longer, Deepak had called Oscar, pleading for help because he simply needed to know what his son was doing.

'I don't mean to violate his privacy, Oscar, but if he is in some kind of trouble, I need to know—simply so that I can help him out,' Deepak had said.

Oscar had thought of Ankit Tripathi and had agreed instantly.

For several days after reaching Mumbai, Oscar had watched Deepak and Rohit's house. The first day, Rohit did nothing but study in his room, and for three days after that, he attended exams in his college and came back home, while Oscar shadowed him in a car that he had borrowed from one of his old friends on the force.

On the last day of his exams, Rohit left from college and went to Girgaum Chowpatty. He sat there for close to four hours, after which he cycled back to college but left from there within five minutes to go home.

Oscar, while watching Rohit at the chowpatty, had seen some vendors pointing at him and laughing. After Rohit went home, Oscar went back to the chowpatty and spoke to the vendors. They told him that the boy was frequently seen at the beach, talking to himself and even making gestures at an imaginary companion. Rohit had become quite popular among the vendors as the boy who was off his rocker.

Oscar's disgust for the city deepened. Any decent human being would have tried to help a kid seen talking to himself on a regular basis. *Not these bastards*, he thought.

He decided to wait and learn more before informing Deepak, and the very next evening, Rohit followed someone to Dadar and then to Tardeo. There, he slipped into an engagement venue, came out again and staked out the place till Anuj came out with a couple who were obviously his parents.

What the hell, Oscar had thought, on recognising Anuj.

Only Oscar saw Rohit slip a kitchen knife out of his knapsack and tuck it into the back of his trousers as he went up to talk to Anuj, and that was when the alarm bells started ringing in Oscar's head.

Quickly, as he slipped out of his car and ran towards the young men, he called up the one person he knew would act first and ask questions later. Patankar, his old friend and batchmate. The brotherhood of batchmates had worked as perfectly as ever. Patankar, who had left from his office, was close to Mumbai Central and got to the hotel within minutes.

'We're here, sir,' the constable from the Agripada Police Station reported to Patankar. After handcuffing Rohit, Patankar had called up the senior inspector of the Agripada Police Station, in whose jurisdiction the hotel fell, and asked for backup to bring Rohit in.

When the group of cops accompanying Rohit arrived at the police station, Oscar opened the door of the police SUV and stepped out, while Anuj stepped out on the other side. Two other constables in the back of the SUV dragged an unconscious Rohit into the police station and straight to the lock-up. Oscar had had to reluctantly hit Rohit on the back of his head to render him unconscious because he wouldn't stop kicking and screaming.

Oscar had called Deepak on the way, and he had already reached the police station. So had Rupa.

A little later, they were all in the senior inspector's cabin.

'You're all lying!' Rohit screamed, struggling like a wild animal to free himself of the handcuffs restraining him.

'Son, please ...' Deepak began, and Rohit whipped around on him.

'*You* stay out of this!' he said. 'You, of all people, do not get to say anything!'

Deepak fell back in his chair, defeated.

'Listen, boy,' Senior Inspector Jairaj Patil said. 'Whatever you say happened, never happened. Okay? Just trust me here.'

'Trust you?' Rohit shouted. 'You people dismissed my mother's death as an accident! Trust you? Really?'

'Rohit ...' Rupa began, and he turned to her. 'Rohit, listen to me. There's been a misunderstanding.'

'Is that what you call it?' Rohit demanded, tears welling up in his eyes. 'A *misunderstanding*? All those ... beautiful ... evenings at the beach? All those times you told me you'll never leave me? And then you go and get engaged to another man?'

Rupa shook her head. 'I don't know what you're talking about, Rohit,' she said sadly.

'Really? Let me make it easy for you, then. Remember what you told me after my mother's death? That if I wanted to talk to you, I could talk to you any time?'

'Yes, I remember that. But ...?'

'And then I came to the staff room and told you I'd be at Girgaum Chowpatty? And you came to meet me the same evening?'

Intersections

There was a deep sadness in Rupa's eyes. 'No, Rohit, you never came to the staff room. And I never met you at the chowpatty.'

Rohit suddenly went limp.

Senior Inspector Patil told Deepak that Anuj and Rupa had decided not to file a complaint, and that his seniors had agreed. Oscar was about to say something, but Patil went on before he could.

'Provided you make sure your son gets psychiatric help,' he told Deepak.

Oscar patted Deepak on the back.

'I'm so sorry,' he said, as Patil turned to leave.

'Mr Patil,' Deepak said. Patil turned back.

'Can you contact my sister and tell her to take custody of Rohit?'

Patil, Patankar and Oscar exchanged looks.

'Why?' Patil asked.

'I'd like to surrender,' Deepak said, staring dejectedly at his feet.

The officers looked mystified.

'For what?' Patankar asked.

'Abetment to suicide,' Deepak replied.

In his hospital room, Rohit woke to find one of his hands cuffed to the bed. He looked up to see Rupa sitting on the bed beside him, a loving smile on her face. He started crying bitterly.

'They say it was all in my head,' Rohit whimpered

like a child. 'They're saying something about delusions. About hallucinations and things.'

'Shhh,' Rupa said, sliding closer to him. 'They don't understand.'

'But you do,' he said, moving as much as the handcuff allowed him to, so that his head was touching her lap. 'Only you do.'

'I'm always here,' she said, stroking his hair. 'Always.'

Through the glass window in the door, Oscar peered in from outside at Rohit curled up on the bed, still hanging onto a beautiful dream which was the only source of happiness in his life.

He knew the feeling.

35

Oscar had learned about Mhatre's suspension from Patankar the previous night and decided to go check on him. The cop in him knew that the suspension was called for, but the human being inside him understood Mhatre, even if he did not condone what he'd done.

He also suspected that, at some level, his narration of the truth behind his own resignation years ago may have pushed Mhatre towards the edge. It was not his fault, of course, but he still wanted to visit Mhatre to see how he was doing.

For a while, the two men talked of other matters, including the strange case of Rohit's alternate reality.

'You're saying he dreamed up an entire love story?' Mhatre asked in wonder.

Oscar nodded.

'How does that even work?' Mhatre asked curiously.

Oscar shrugged. 'I don't know. It's psychiatric stuff. Who understands all that? Apparently, Rohit's mind was already fragile after his mother's suicide and latched onto his teacher, who he had always liked, the minute she showed him sympathy. The hope for something more with her did the rest, from what I could understand.'

'Who was it who said, hope is a dangerous thing?' Mhatre asked.

'I don't know who originally said it,' Oscar replied, 'but I remember Morgan Freeman's character saying it in *The Shawshank Redemption*.'

Mhatre stuck a cigarette in his mouth and offered one to Oscar, who held up his hand. 'I'm trying to cut down,' he said. 'My smoking has gone way up after I came here.'

'I don't blame you,' Mhatre said as he lit up.

Oscar studied Mhatre as he smoked, standing near the window. Outwardly, he seemed fine. The matter of his suspension was the elephant in the room that they hadn't acknowledged yet, and it was sure to come up at some point. But all things considered, Mhatre seemed to be taking it well.

'Want to come with me to see him?' Oscar asked on a whim.

'Who, the kid?' Mhatre said, startled at the offer.

'I'm going to visit him. Just to check how he's doing.'

'I don't know, sir …'

'Come on, it'll take your mind off things.'

Mhatre didn't say anything to that.

Intersections

'It's better than sitting here and getting drunk, you know ...' Oscar smiled sardonically at the memory of their previous binge together.

Mhatre responded with a chuckle and stubbed out his cigarette. An hour later, they were pulling up in the parking lot of the mental health facility in Dadar on Mhatre's bike.

The word that came to Mhatre's mind when he first saw Rohit was 'broken'. He didn't know what the boy had looked like earlier, but as Rohit sat down in front of him and Oscar in the lobby, there was a vacant look in his eyes and the corners of his mouth were turned downwards.

Before meeting him, they had met the doctor, who said that he was on medication to keep the delusions at bay, but the problem was that he wasn't ready to let them go yet. He would need prolonged therapy sessions before he could take that step.

'How're you, Rohit?' Oscar asked with a slight smile.

Rohit shrugged uncertainly.

'It's ... I just ... I'm not sure what's real anymore,' he said. 'One minute Rupa is sitting next to me, and the next minute I suddenly realise that the person I see isn't there. It's confusing.'

'This is my friend, Uday,' Oscar said.

Mhatre smiled at him and offered his hand. Rohit took it uncertainly and shook it once before letting go.

'Has anyone from your family been to see you?' Oscar asked.

Rohit nodded. 'My aunt comes every day. But we're not exactly close. The doctor says I'll need to stay here for some more time. It's ... it's frustrating, but I guess I get why it's required.'

'You like to read, Rohit?' Mhatre asked. The boy nodded again.

'Can I get you some books next time I come?'

Oscar looked at him.

'Well, the thing is,' Uday continued, 'Mr Fernandes here will be leaving for home soon, and I thought I'd keep you company in his absence. If you're fine with it, of course.'

Rohit shrugged. 'I guess,' he said, with a teenager's typical show of nonchalance.

'I read a lot when I was your age,' Mhatre said, smiling.

Rohit was silent. Both Oscar and Mhatre realised that he was struggling to get something out.

'I can't stop thinking about one thing,' he said finally. 'If Rupa ... if none of it was real ... if she never came to meet me at the beach ever ... why ... why did that girl say she saw her?'

The men exchanged looks. Their cop instincts were immediately switched on.

'What girl, buddy?' Oscar asked.

'This ... this young girl. Must be Rupa's age. I'd seen her at the beach before. She took walks in the evening. The day I learned about the engagement, I waited at the beach for ages, thinking she'd come. This girl was there and she asked me if something was wrong. We got talking about Rupa.'

Oscar nodded. He had seen the girl have a short conversation with Rohit before leaving the beach.

'She ... I asked if she'd seen Rupa that evening, and she said no, but she'd seen us on other evenings ... and how happy I had looked with her.'

Oscar was trying to remember what the girl looked like. He had only seen her from a distance, and his charge was Rohit, so he hadn't paid too much attention to her, because she didn't seem like a threat to the boy.

'She also told me that the world is an ugly place, and that I should guard my happiness fiercely. Those were her exact words. That's ... that' s why I decided to ... you know, do what I did ...'

'I know, I know,' Oscar said soothingly.

'Did ... Did I imagine her as well?' Rohit looked really scared.

Oscar leaned forward and laid a hand on his shoulder.

'Rohit,' he said. 'I was watching you that day. And no, you didn't imagine her. I saw her too.'

'You ... you did, right? She was there!'

'Tell you what,' Mhatre said. 'We'll try to find her. Try to clear this up. What do you say?'

Rohit nodded eagerly.

The doctor arrived. 'Shall we go, Rohit?' he asked gently. 'You have a session scheduled now.'

Rohit stood up silently.

'Just one thing,' Mhatre said as he and Oscar got up to leave. 'What did she look like?'

Rohit thought for a moment. 'Small face. Her entire frame was small, actually. Hair up to her shoulder with green ... highlights? Is that what they're called?'

Mhatre nodded.

'A nose-pin. And small earrings.'

An hour later, Mhatre and Oscar were at the police chowky at the Girgaum Chowpatty. The sub-inspector in charge of the chowky wasn't exactly comfortable helping them, in the light of Mhatre's recent disgrace, but they patiently explained to him how a young boy was involved and that their desire to know more about him was completely above-board. Ultimately, the PSI agreed to let them view the CCTV footage of the day Rohit had met the woman.

Oscar made him fast-forward it till he saw the woman approach Rohit.

'Okay, now let's forward it again to the point when she leaves him. I want to see where she goes,' Mhatre said.

The PSI obeyed and after five to six minutes, the girl turned away from Rohit, came up to the main road, passing by the camera, and went out of sight.

'Any cameras facing the beach?'

The PSI nodded and switched through cameras till he found the right one. It captured the woman crossing the street after leaving the beach.

'Stop,' Mhatre said, and the PSI froze the video.

The woman was pretty close to the camera and the quality of the image was much better than what it used to be when the Mumbai Police first started using CCTV cameras. Small frame, shoulder-length hair, green highlights.

Mhatre took out his phone and carefully took a close-up picture of the still.

'Thanks for this, yaar,' he said to the PSI. 'Don't worry. No one will know.'

The PSI nodded but said nothing.

Mhatre and Oscar left quickly and got on his bike.

'We could come back here tomorrow and see if she shows up,' Oscar suggested.

'Yeah, but not before evening,' Mhatre said. 'The CM is inaugurating new patrol boats here. The whole place will be crawling with cops till afternoon.'

As he kick-started the bike, a thought nagged at him.

He knew that face.

36

'Boss, the Shivaji Park job was bad enough. I'm not getting involved with you again. The cops got on my ass and the attention was bad for business. And what you're asking for this time is even worse!'

Bhatia was at the window, his back to her.

'That's not the point! And I don't care what you're offering me. I'm done with you. Don't call me again.'

He disconnected the call without listening to the other person's reply and turned around to see her at the door. She hardly ever made any sound, and he was almost always taken by surprise to see her standing or sitting near him.

'Shivaji Park. That was you?' she asked.

He nodded absently.

Chhaya saw that he was using a different phone, one that he didn't usually make calls with. She watched carefully as Bhatia placed it in a drawer in the cabinet near his bed.

'Hello, beautiful,' Sanika said adoringly, slipping into bed beside her.

'You have to stop startling me like that,' she sighed, turning to face her.

'I can't help it.' Sanika giggled. 'You're too cute when you are startled.'

'Bitch,' she whispered in Sanika's ear. They kissed.

'I'm taking the day off tomorrow,' Sanika said, and an alarm went off in Chhaya's head.

'Why?' she asked, raising herself on her elbows.

'It's a Friday. I thought we could go away somewhere and come back on Sunday night. What say?'

Chhaya thought fast. 'But I won't be here, darling,' she said.

Sanika's face fell.

'Why not?' she looked crushed.

'Ummm ...' Chhaya sat up in bed.

'Jolene, what's wrong?' Sanika asked.

'Nothing ... nothing's wrong, as such. But ... okay, this is embarrassing. Remember I told you I'm here on family business?'

Sanika nodded.

'I've inherited some money from a relative who's passed away. It's ... it's quite a significant amount and I'm still getting used to the idea of having that much money, which is why I didn't tell you. It's embarrassing.'

'Okaaaay ...'

'So, I have to complete the legal formalities tomorrow. It's going to be a lengthy process and there will be other inheritors and stuff. And it's all the way in Andheri.'

Sanika slid closer to her.

'I'm so sorry,' she said. 'You should have told me that you lost someone in the family. I had no idea.'

'Oh, no, no. It's not like we were close or anything. Just that he ... my uncle ... didn't have any kids and he held my father in high regard, so I guess that's why he left me all that money. I don't know.'

Sanika still looked disappointed.

'I'm sorry,' Chhaya said, caressing her cheek. 'I should have told you earlier.'

'It's okay,' Sanika said, attempting a small smile. 'I'll tell the office I'm coming in to work after all. You and I can do what I'd planned some other time.'

'Saturday,' Chhaya said. 'We'll go somewhere on Saturday and come back on Sunday. All expenses paid by your newly rich girlfriend!'

Sanika laughed and hugged her. Chhaya slid backwards till her back was resting against the wall and pulled Sanika close so that her head was in her lap. Sanika curled up and purred like a contented kitten.

Inwardly, Chhaya sighed with relief. Sanika at home tomorrow was the last thing she needed. She only had a small window and was not going to miss it. Sanika usually left quite early in the morning, so she would not be around to check if Chhaya had really gone to Andheri.

This was not exactly her area of expertise. Which was why she had let Bhatia plan it to the last detail.

'Sophisticated sniper rifles are for movies,' Bhatia had told her. *'In an urban landscape, where everything is closely packed together, any decent assault rifle with a normal scope is enough. Success lies in the aim, when even wind velocity does not matter — if the distance isn't too great.'*

'How do you know all this?'

Bhatia only smiled. Her guess was that he had served in the armed forces. Or knew someone who had.

She had identified Sanika's house as the ideal one almost as soon as she saw it from the beach three months ago, when Bhatia first sent her for a recon run. She spent the next two months learning everything she could about its owner. Sanika Grover was single and lonely, and that she was a lesbian was a welcome coincidence. Till she had orchestrated that meeting with Sanika, and things had worked out the way they had, Chhaya had had a host of contingency plans, including slipping into the building on the day of the mission and forcing her way into the house at gunpoint.

Bhatia, meanwhile, got in touch with his contact at the ordnance factory and roped in Gurpreet Singh and Niyaz Ansari to handle the delivery.

Everything was in place.

The only thing Bhatia had been against was her manning the gun.

'Look, I don't doubt you can do this, but the entire state's police force will be after you before you know it,' he had said.

'How will they even know who to look for?' she'd argued. 'And I'll be gone the same day. We'll plan the entire exit in detail. No one will even know you were in the city, and you can leave a day earlier. I'll escape in the initial chaos and be on a flight by the time they figure out where to look.'

Bhatia still had his reservations but ultimately he agreed, simply because using Chhaya was his best option. It cut out the need for using history-sheeters, who were sure to be picked up—and not many were available for something so daring, anyway. The best thing about the assignment was that no one was supposed to get hurt. The job was audacious and was going to have far-reaching consequences, which was exactly the client's intention.

Once all the planning was done and the gun had left the ordnance factory, to be delivered to Mumbai through a circuitous route, Bhatia became redundant. As a precautionary measure, in the light of the police's heightened interest in Ansari, she had asked him to hold on to the gun and had only taken delivery of it at Sanika's house two days earlier. Bhatia had tutored her on how to assemble it, and she could always consult the ever-informative internet if she needed to. Sanika would leave early enough to give her time to attend to all that.

Intersections

She was glad that she had averted the small threat to her plan. The alternative would have been to kill Sanika.

Earlier in the night, she had watched from the living room window as the cops arrived at the chowpatty across the street from Sanika's house, to make sure the place was secure for the next day's event. She had made several dry runs through the day, and the line of sight was perfect.

Her flight tickets were booked, and she had an entire set of forged identity papers waiting for her where she was going. By the time Sanika came back from work tomorrow, her entire world would be transformed.

She slid back lower on the bed to take Sanika in her arms.

'I'd like to make up for disappointing you,' she whispered.

'That won't be easy,' Sanika whispered back.

'Watch me.'

37

Mhatre was pacing the room, waiting desperately for the information he had requested.

The night of his suspension, he had gone on a binge that had scared even him, despite all the justifications that he was usually able to come up with for his addiction. He had given the bar a miss, afraid that he would end up punching someone in the face if they so much as looked at him wrongly, and had instead picked up a bottle of Scotch from a wine shop on his way home.

One of the rules that he had put in place to keep a check on his drinking was that he would not drink at home. He had hoped that the fact that he had the trip home to make would discourage him from drinking more than he could handle. Like any addict, however, he also found a way around his own rule. Once he discovered that the bar manager would call him a taxi, and that the payment could be taken care of later, any restraint in his drinking went out of the window.

Intersections

He had just started paying for his drinks, however. The shame of binging on free alcohol was eating at him from the inside. As a result, he was running out of spending money and would soon have to dip into his savings.

The night he got home after the suspension order was handed him, he sat in the living room with the bottle in front of him and started drinking slowly, peg by peg, not caring about the measure. There was nothing to eat in the house because Mhatre didn't cook and ate most of his meals on the go. He hadn't bothered to pick anything up and was in no mood for food, anyway.

When he woke up the next morning, he was sprawled out on the floor somewhere between the bathroom and the living room, with no memory of how he had ended up there. The fact that he was facing away from the bathroom indicated that he had been on his way back after relieving himself, and the absence of any bruises on his body signified that he had not fallen, or not fallen hard.

Slowly, he stood up, his head pounding hard and his throat so dry that he was unable to utter a sound. The bottle of Scotch was three-fourths empty and he seemed to have smoked an entire pack of cigarettes, the half-smoked remainder of one of them lying under the table in the living room. Again, he had no memory of how that had happened.

As he thirstily chugged down an entire bottle of water, he felt a slight tremor in his hands even as he tried to grip the bottle tightly.

Shakily, he went to the bedroom and collapsed on the bed, where he slept till afternoon, when Oscar came by. The rest of his day was taken care of, thanks to Oscar and Rohit and the mysterious girl with the green highlights in her hair, but the night proved the real nemesis.

After the previous night, he had decided to give his body a rest. As a result, he spent half the night tossing and turning, fighting the urge to finish the remaining Scotch in the bottle, before he passed out from exhaustion.

He woke up with a start the next morning, his tortured dreams suddenly throwing up a face at him from nowhere. His heart was pounding and he was sweating all over.

Hastily, he reached for his phone and called up an old friend in the Shivaji Park Police Station.

'Are you crazy?' the PI exclaimed. 'I mean, no offence, Mhatre, but you're an untouchable right now. I shouldn't even have taken your call.'

'Sir, please, sir. This is not even connected to the reason I was suspended. And if my lead pans out, it could be huge. I will turn over all the information to you if it does, and you can take over the matter officially. I promise.'

Intersections

There was silence.

'I'll see what I can do.'

'It's really urgent, sir ...'

'I said I'll see what I can do, Mhatre,' the PI said curtly, and hung up.

That had been an hour ago and Mhatre was pacing restlessly, waiting to hear back from the PI, when there was a knock at the door. He went to open it, expecting Oscar or Patankar.

What he had never expected was to see Niyaz Ansari standing outside his door.

Instinctively, his hand went to the back of his waistband before he remembered that he had had to surrender his service weapon following his suspension. Ansari, however, shrank back in fright and raised both hands.

'I ... I just want to talk, sir. Please, sir. Let me at least come inside.'

Mhatre realised that the fear on Ansari's face was not caused by him. He had already been scared before Mhatre opened the door.

He stepped back and let Ansari enter, and the first thing he did after shutting the door—which he did without turning his back to Ansari—was to thoroughly search him for a weapon.

'*Maarke rakh di meri, saale,*' he said, waving him to a chair at the table.

'Sir, I didn't do anything, sir. I don't even know

who took that video. I ran away as soon as I had a chance.'

'What are you doing here?' Mhatre asked roughly.

'I ... she'll kill me, sir!'

'She?'

'That woman. The one in the burqa. I'm sure she's going to kill me.'

Mhatre took a deep breath and forced himself to calm down, reminding himself that he had been suspended because of his own stupidity. He went to the kitchen and came back with a glass of water.

'You were delivering something for Bhatia, weren't you?' he asked, handing him the glass. 'She was with him?'

Ansari nodded before draining the glass. Then he sighed deeply before speaking again.

'I swear, I didn't even look inside the package. But it was big. And heavy. If there was a gun in there, it is a big gun. Definitely not a handgun. I took it from some fellow in Nagpur three days ago, kept it with me and delivered it the same day that you ... you came for me.'

'Why would she kill you, then?'

'She is one scary woman, sir! All through, she told me multiple times that she would kill me if I talked to the cops.'

'And here you are,' Mhatre said. 'Why? What can you tell me about her?'

'I think she killed Bhatia. And she would have killed Gurpreet Singh too, had she not cut him out of the job.'

'She did that?' Mhatre asked.

'Sir, as soon as Bhatia died, she took over completely. Before that, she hardly spoke a word. But after his death, she told me that something had changed. That I was now supposed to pick up a different package three days later than what was planned. And she told me very clearly that if I attracted any police attention, she would kill me. But you were already on my trail and I knew you'd never give up the hunt.'

'That's why you got Siddiqui to file that complaint, didn't you?'

'Sir, you haven't been in the same room with her. I have. It's like she has no feelings of any kind. That's why I'm scared. Now that my work is done, she's going to bump me off.'

'But you haven't even seen her face!' Mhatre said. The unending whine was beginning to irritate him.

'But sir, she knows I have seen her friend's face. The one I delivered the package to. I know she wouldn't take the chance of my blabbing a description of her. Whatever she's doing today is too big ...'

'Wait, she's doing it today?'

'She ... she said everything has to be in place before today ... she was very firm about it ...'

Mhatre sprang out of his seat and ran to get his phone. He meant to call Patankar, but as he unlocked the screen, he saw a WhatsApp message from the PI at Shivaji Park. It was an image file. With trembling fingers he opened it and started at it silently, aware of an increase in his heartbeat.

'Sir ...?' said Ansari, noticing the expression on his face.

Mhatre kept staring at the screen, unable to believe his eyes.

'Sir ...'

Mhatre shook off his shock and asked the first question that came to mind.

'This friend you delivered the package to ...' he asked Ansari. 'Who was it?'

'Some girl, sir. Really young. Weird, too. Her hair was half-green.'

Mhatre looked up from his phone, his head starting to spin a little.

38

'Who was it? On the phone?'

Bhatia looked at her hard before answering. She had already guessed that he was beginning to trust her more and more. And even if he didn't, she was prepared to torture the information out of him.

'Tell me,' she said.

Bhatia took a second or two to respond.

'Chintan Mehta,' he said eventually.

Chhaya slid the last part of the MP5 sub-machine gun in place. Only the ammunition clip remained to be inserted. She aimed the gun out of the window and squeezed the trigger. The sound it made told her that the weapon seemed to be in proper working condition. She squeezed the trigger several more times, listening for the sounds of the hammer, before laying it aside.

As she went about preparing for the day that she had worked so hard towards, she was thinking of the conversation with Bhatia that had set the entire sequence of events into motion.

'You're joking,' she said.

'I wish I was,' Bhatia replied. 'There are people who will say I am a bad guy. But fuckers like him are pure evil.'

'But why would he do that?'

Chhaya realised it was the first time in years that she had actually felt shock and surprise.

'Pure evil,' Bhatia repeated. 'Remember how he shot to fame? Helping victims of fires because he said he'd lost his father in one? The fucker arranged for that fire so he could inherit his fortune before time. Me, I just deliver weapons. That bastard, he's the devil himself.'

'But why kill those innocents at Shivaji Park?'

'Think,' Bhatia said. 'Who gained the most from it? Who, in fact, was the only one who gained from it? He himself. He became a hero. From a philanthropist, he became target practice for people of ill intent. He got sympathy by the fucking tonne. His business went up. His popularity went up. The government became his friend. Half the contracts he got for years after that were because no one would want to turn him down.'

He broke off and looked thoughtful. 'He paid a bloody barrel of money for that grenade.'

'How much?'

'One-and-a-half crore,' Bhatia replied. 'Didn't even hesitate when I asked for it.'

Chhaya took a moment. This was too much even for her.
'What does he want now?' she asked.
Bhatia told her.
'And you're serious about not doing the job?'
'He's evil, Chhaya,' he said once again. 'He'll stop at nothing. Only, this time his instructions are that nobody is supposed to get hurt.'
'How much is he offering?'
'What? No! I'm not doing this. Where will he even find someone willing to do something like this?'
'How much?'
Bhatia hesitated.
'Ten crore.'
'Take it.'
'Did you not hear me? Nobody is going to put themselves on the line to …'
'I'll do it.'

Chhaya reached into the package and came out with the ammunition clip and the box of 9 x 19 mm parabellum rounds. She started filling out the clip, round by round.

'Look, I don't doubt you can do this, but the entire state's police force will be behind you before you know it,' Bhatia said.
'How will they even know who to look for?' she argued. 'And I'll be gone the same day. We'll plan the entire exit in

detail. No one will even know you were in the city, and you can leave a day earlier. I'll escape in the initial chaos and be on a flight by the time they figure out where to look.'

'Why do you want to do this so badly?'

'For us,' she replied. *'That money will help us go legitimate forever. We'll invest in some business and be done with people like Chintan Mehta forever. We can even move somewhere else.'*

Bhatia pondered her words silently.

'You're not getting any younger. And I have an entire life ahead of me that I would like to enjoy,' she said.

Finally, Bhatia nodded. 'Okay, but at the first sign that tells me this is too dangerous, I'm cancelling the job.'

She nodded and stood up to leave.

At the door, she turned around again.

'Thank you,' she said.

Bhatia looked at her. 'For what?'

'For all that you've done for me. I really mean it.'

Bhatia looked at her curiously, but he was used to her suddenly saying things that didn't make sense. He only nodded.

She turned around and left the room. She could hardly tell him at that point that she might not get to say those words again before she killed him.

She slammed the ammunition clip home and raised the gun, putting her eye to the scope. It was not a very high-powered scope, but it was enough. Sanika's apartment was in a building located behind the row of buildings directly across the street from the chowpatty. Her living room window offered a direct line of sight through a gap between two buildings on the main road.

In case of any attack, the police would first check the buildings across the street. That much time was enough for her to make a clean getaway.

Immediately after Bhatia's death, she had used his phone to call his contact in the ordnance factory to ask for one last component. A silencer. That was also when she had discovered that Bhatia recorded all his calls. Including the one with Chintan Mehta.

She took the silencer out of the package now and screwed it on to the barrel. Mehta's orders had been to hurt no one, but to make a lot of noise. He was in for a reversal of his own instructions. Especially when the bullets from her silenced gun hit him.

She turned to the window, taking care to stay out of sight, and raised the scope to her eyes again. Bhatia had been right. In urban scenarios, any decent gun with a normal scope was enough. Sophisticated sniper rifles with high-powered scopes were for the movies.

The enhanced sight that the scope nevertheless gave her allowed her to observe the events at the chowpatty. It was teeming with policemen and the dignitaries were set to arrive any second.

Fucking finally, she thought.

At that instant, there was a series of loud noises as the front door was kicked open. She whirled around, the MP5 ready to fire, and saw a man armed with a handgun burst through the door.

Shit, she thought.

She knew him only too well.

'Tanisha!' API Uday Mhatre shouted. 'Tanisha, I just want to talk!'

39

She had recently turned nineteen and had lived at the shelter home since as long as she could remember. It was the nuns who had given her the name Tanisha.

She had jumped over the low compound wall to join her friends because the Chintan Mehta, the person she had read and heard so much about, was going to be at the playground just some minutes away. She had no way of knowing that someone was going to be lobbing a grenade at him.

Even as the attacker turned to flee, she stood rooted to the spot, her ears ringing from the force of the explosion. The shock wave had rendered her immobile. Through a haze, she saw a uniformed cop get up from where he had fallen, his face lined with soot and blood, aim his gun and shoot the attacker in the back of his head.

Half the face disappeared in a spray of blood and brain. As he fell, she was bathed in most of it.

The red film over her eyes seemed to mock at all the lessons that she had learned about love, compassion, mercy and other such things. The world was not a beautiful place glowing with the glory of love and the Lord. The world was ugly, and she had its blood on her face. She opened her mouth to scream and tasted the killer's blood. She didn't know it then, but she'd never be able to close her eyes without having that same feeling for years after that.

Through the red haze, she saw the young policeman, still standing with his gun raised, for a very long second.

Their eyes locked, and for one moment, during which time itself seemed to hold its breath, they were the only ones standing still in the middle of the pandemonium around them.

Then, even as she watched, he fell to the ground.

'It's you, isn't it?' Mhatre asked.

She did not lower her gun but slowly, unwillingly, she nodded.

'How did you know?' she asked.

'Rohit?' Mhatre said. 'The boy you met at the chowpatty the other day?'

Chhaya didn't say anything for a minute. She remembered the boy because she had recognised another soul as broken as hers, but she hadn't found out his name. Her brain was struggling to connect what was happening now to a random encounter with a teenager to whom she had lied, simply to keep his beautiful illusion alive.

'What does he have to do with any of this?' she snapped.

'Look, Tanisha, just come with me, okay? Put the gun down, and come with me. I swear I'll tell you everything.'

'No,' she said.

Mhatre thought hard and fast. The window she was standing at gave her a direct line of sight to the chowpatty. Slowly, carefully, he took one step to his right, stepping further inside the house. She instinctively took a step behind and to her left to stay face to face with him, and in the process moved away from the window.

'Listen! Listen to me. I made some inquiries. There was a missing persons complaint filed for you after you disappeared that night. The same night that the incident occurred. And I'm sorry. I'm so, *so* sorry that no one seems to have looked for you hard enough. And I'm so sorry that what happened at Shivaji Park affected you enough to make you run away. Look where you ended up!'

'I kept seeing blood every time I closed my eyes,' she said quietly.

Mhatre took another step to his right. She took one more to her left.

'I can't even imagine your horror,' Mhatre said. 'I can't. We should have tried harder to find you so that we could help you. But the truth is that we didn't. Let me try and make that right. Please, Tanisha.'

'You have no idea what happened *after* that,' she said. 'You have no idea where life led me.'

'I don't,' Mhatre agreed. 'I don't. Just come with me, please? Tell me everything? We'll sort this out together. I'm so, so sorry, Tanisha.'

'None of what happened that day was your fault, Mhatre,' Tanisha said.

'It was,' Mhatre said in a strangled voice, as if he was trying hard not to cry. 'It was!'

Hidden beyond the doorframe, his own gun in his hands, Patankar was listening intently. It was a strategy they had both agreed on while on the way up to the fourth-floor flat. That Mhatre would go in first, because he knew who Chhaya really was, and Patankar would be the backup.

Immediately after the conversation with Ansari, Mhatre had called up Patankar. He was in the squad office at the time.

'Uday, I swear to God …'

'Sir, listen to me,' Mhatre said, already on his bike and ready to take off. 'Niyaz Ansari came to me, okay? He stood in my house and spilled his guts out. I'm willing to bet that the woman who took the package is the same one we're looking for, and the address he gave me is in Girgaum, bang opposite the chowpatty.'

'Girgaum Chowpatty? But the CM is inaugurating the new speedboats there in …'

'In half an hour, I know. And there's more. But we haven't the time for that. I'm going there, sir. And I really need backup.'

'*Bhenchod!*' Patankar said, already out of his chair. 'I'm coming. *Do not* go in alone.'

He had unlocked the cabinet in his office where he kept the spare guns, taken a pistol out along with a magazine and a box of 9 mm rounds, and run out of his cabin.

'Come on,' he said to a startled Kadam, shoving the pistol and ammunition in her hands.

She loaded her weapon on the way as they sped in the police car to Girgaum.

'Sir!' Patankar was yelling into his phone, which he had placed on speaker mode on the dashboard. 'I swear I will explain everything to you. For now, please don't let the CM, or any other VIP, close to Girgaum Chowpatty.'

There was a pause.

'Is this you or is this Mhatre?' DCP Samad Khan asked.

'This is me, sir,' Patankar said, without hesitating. 'This is all me.'

They met at the entrance to the building, Mhatre pulling up on his bike at the same time that Patankar and Kadam zoomed up in the unmarked car that the squad used for covert operations.

Mhatre had his cellphone out.

'This is our target,' he said, showing them a photograph on his cellphone. It was the CCTV still of Chhaya he had taken from the Girgaum chowky.

'Wait,' Kadam said, looking at it. 'That's our girl! The hair and make-up is different but she is the same woman who checked into the Bandra hotel!'

'So the Bandra connection did pan out, huh?' Mhatre said, pulling a gun out of his waistband. It was his licensed personal weapon, one which he had obtained after the Shivaji Park incident. His seniors had advised him to get one, in light of the fact that he had shot down the attacker.

'Shut up, you smug bastard,' Patankar said, as he and Kadam pulled out their own weapons. 'Cover the exit,' he told Kadam. 'That girl comes out, you shoot first and ask questions later.'

Kadam nodded.

'Don't hesitate,' Mhatre told her. 'From personal experience, just don't. If she comes out of the building, it means she's killed both of us. Just shoot.'

'I got this, Uday,' Kadam said, crossing the lane. The society had two gates, several feet apart, and being on the other side of the lane gave her a better vantage point.

Now, with her MP5 sub-machine gun still half-trained on Mhatre, Chhaya asked, 'How was it your fault? You shot the fucker down.'

'I froze,' Mhatre said.

It was a hazard that all of Mhatre's instructors had warned him about at the Academy.

'The very first time you will need to fire your weapon,' they had cautioned, 'you will never be sure if it's right to do it. And you will be overwhelmed by fear for your personal safety. There will be a lot of reasons to hesitate. The yardstick is simple. Your actions can either save lives or cost lives. If this knowledge can overcome your concern for staying alive, you're good.'

'I was afraid,' Mhatre said. 'I ... I had spotted the bomber way earlier. But even as he was reaching into his arm sling for the grenade, I was thinking about my own safety. What if he had a gun? What if I tried to accost him and he shot me? By the time I did raise an alarm, he had already pulled the pin from the grenade. Whatever happened after that was as much my fault as anyone else's.'

With a sinking feeling in his heart, Patankar realised that this was what Mhatre had been about to tell him that evening outside Khan's office. And that this was why the Shivaji Park incident had affected him so much. The drinking, the recklessness, it all suddenly started making sense.

'It's been five years and that thought still haunts me, Tanisha,' Mhatre said. 'A few seconds of hesitation, and now I have the blood of five innocents on my hands. I still hear their names in my head. I am responsible for their deaths as much as anyone else. And I have lived with that every second of the last five years.'

Patankar thumbed down the safety catch of his service weapon. Mhatre was getting emotional and that was absolutely the worst thing one could do in the middle of an ongoing operation.

Chhaya was silent for a long moment, while Patankar waited, his back to the wall, ready to move in.

'If that is true,' she said finally, 'you deserve to die as much as Chintan Mehta does.'

'Chintan Mehta?' Mhatre asked even as she pointed the sub-machine gun at him.

Patankar had heard enough. He knew a death knell when he heard it.

He left his post and swivelled around, gun raised.

From her post outside the building, Kadam heard two rapid gunshots. She ran to the car they had come in and grabbed the wireless radio.

40

It would be a week before the dust around what the news media were already calling the 'Girgaum Shootout' would begin to settle.

The urgent alert that Kadam had sent out from outside the building was picked up by all the policemen across the street. The DCP in charge of security had already been informed by Khan that Mehta and the CM were not coming, and he promptly diverted all the manpower to the building. It took less than a minute for the cops to come running, guns drawn, and as soon as she saw the first of them, Kadam rushed inside.

She reached the fourth floor and looked around. Thanks to the gunshots, the entire building was agog. All the doors were open and people were peeking outside gingerly to see what had happened.

'Get back inside, you idiots!' she ordered, and three out of the four doors on the floor were quickly slammed shut. She ran to the fourth door, gun raised.

Mhatre was standing with his gun still at eye-level. She followed his line of sight to the woman sprawled on the floor. There was a silenced MP5 sub-machine gun metres away from her.

Carefully, Kadam advanced till she had a better view. The woman's face was partially blown away, but the hair, and the green highlights, were visible. The woman was very obviously dead.

The threat had been neutralised.

She turned around to see Patankar behind her, looking at Mhatre with a mix of pride and wonder.

'Didn't hesitate for even a blink,' he commented. 'Not one blink. I think we just got our boy back.'

Mhatre lowered his gun with trembling hands. Then he collapsed on his knees, lowered his head and cried like he had never cried in his life.

Patankar went outside as more cops came running up. He held up a hand and made them wait while Kadam helped get Mhatre back in control.

Uday Mhatre took a series of deep breaths before wiping his face and rising to his feet. Then he went to look for the bathroom while Patankar let the other cops inside.

The aftermath, as could be expected, was chaotic. All sorts of agencies descended on the scene, followed shortly by the politicians. The CP himself came down to take stock.

The entire lane was cordoned off as the news media gathered in droves. Khan, who was among the first to get to the scene, had had the good sense to take Mhatre, Kadam and Patankar away in the first available police vehicle, before the madness started. Patankar remembered only too well the consequences of encounter specialists strutting about the scenes of their encounters, guns tucked into their waistbands in full view, shooting their mouths off on camera. That era had been put an end to for a reason.

Mhatre's phone was ringing almost constantly, but he hadn't the energy or desire to talk to anyone. As it was a police shooting, Crime Branch Unit II started an inquiry. The three cops were driven to the unit office at Saat Rasta Circle. The PI in charge of Unit II, Bharat Gune, took an initial statement needed for the registration of the FIR and then left Mhatre alone in an inner room.

Patankar and Kadam hung around to back him up for any contingencies. Mhatre had taken the shot for the right reasons. Now it was the police force's job to take care of their own.

Bang in the middle of it, Niyaz Ansari turned up at the Unit II office, causing a minor commotion. Patankar spotted him and allowed him inside.

'Sir, when do I record my confession? *Abhi karu?*'

Patankar spoke to an officer, who led Ansari away. Ansari paused just once before leaving.

'Thank you, sir,' he said to Mhatre, who only nodded.

It was night by the time Khan came to the unit office and sat down in a chair next to Mhatre.

'I'm sorry, sir,' Mhatre said before Khan could say anything. 'For all the times I …'

'It's okay, Mhatre,' Khan said. 'Patankar told me what went on in that house. He told me about the Shivaji Park incident.'

Mhatre said nothing.

Khan leaned back in his seat.

'This job …' he said. 'It's not supposed to be easy. The entrance exam and training period don't come close to helping us earn the uniform. We earn it on the job.'

'As I am learning, sir,' Mhatre said.

'The last time, you had a lot of fame thrust on you without expecting it. I might not agree with the way you handled it, but your intentions were right. I'm willing to overlook a lot for that reason. This time, however, is your real test.'

'I'll do the best I can, sir.'

'I'm sure you will. And Mhatre, we all experience failure. Every single cop in the force has at some point fallen short in people's — or his own — eyes in some way or the other. But we don't have to deal with it alone. That's what it means to be part of a uniformed force.'

Mhatre looked at Khan.

'Thank you, sir.'

Khan patted Mhatre's shoulder and stood up. Mhatre stood up too.

'Take the week off. Visit your parents. Come meet me when you're back.'

'Yes, sir.'

Khan left and Patankar entered a minute later. He opened the window and then fished out his pack of cigarettes.

'So, how did you know?' Patankar asked. 'How did you know it was her?'

'Hers was the last face I saw at Shivaji Park before I passed out. She was so young and so ... terrified. She had all that blood on her face and she was frozen in shock. It's not an expression you forget. Just that the deaths, and my own failure, affected me so much that I guess I ended up locking her face away in some corner of my head.'

Quickly, he brought Patankar up to speed about his conversation with Rohit and where it led him and Oscar.

'Took me an entire night of sobriety, but I finally remembered. I wasn't sure, so I got a picture of her from when the nuns at the shelter home filed a missing person report on her at Shivaji Park. Five years had passed but I could still recognise the face, despite the hair and all.'

'All roads lead back to Shivaji Park, huh?'

'I can't help thinking that,' Mhatre replied. 'Every tragedy leaves a trail of broken people in its wake. We think it's just one event in one individual's life, but in effect, many people are damaged by it. Me, Tanisha, Oscar, Rohit, even his father. Even that teacher of his. You think she'll ever forget Rohit? And experience guilt—however irrational—over his condition?'

'Life is *about* damage, Uday,' Patankar said, taking a last drag at his cigarette. 'But more importantly, it is about how we deal with it. Our bodies start to decay almost from the moment we're born, but we produce new cells to replace the ones that are dead. That's how we need to approach life as well.'

'Sir,' Mhatre said, looking at the ground.

'*Bol na.*'

'Please go back to turning my favourite songs into jokes. I can't handle all this serious stuff from you.'

'*Chup, gandu!*'

41

'No, no. No one has to die this time. It's a beach! Lots of open sky to aim at. Just make a lot of noise. I'll pay you ten crore. How does that sound? You can retire with that money. You can move abroad!'

'Boss, the Shivaji Park job was bad enough. I'm not getting involved with you again. The cops got on my ass and the attention was bad for business. And what you're asking for this time is even worse!'

'First of all, Shivaji Park was necessary. It worked wonders for me! And you got rich. And as I told you, those people were never supposed to die!'

'That's not the point! And I don't care what you're offering me. I'm done with you. Don't call me again.'

Mhatre watched the news at his parents' home with increasing disbelief as the audio clip was played again and again on the news channel. He reached for the remote and switched through the channels. Every one of them was running the same story. He scrambled for his phone and it started buzzing. It was Patankar.

'You saw the news?' Mhatre asked at once.

'I did,' Patankar replied. 'The CP got in touch with some of the channels. It was emailed to them this morning. We got a copy of the email. The email id is "tanisha.chhaya", whatever the second word is supposed to mean.'

'But ... she's dead!'

Kadam's voice came on the line.

'Uday, you're on speaker. All email service-providers now have the option of scheduling your emails.'

'What does that mean?'

'It means you can compose an email and enter a day and time at which you want it to be sent to its recipients. Tanisha must have scheduled the email to be sent a week after she was supposed to kill Mehta. At least that's what the email says, that Mehta will be dead by the time this email is sent out.'

Tanisha's last words suddenly started making sense to Mhatre.

Oscar walked into the room. Mhatre held up a hand and continued talking.

'But why a week after? Why not immediately? Why not just release this, instead of killing him?'

'Only she could have answered that. As to why not immediately, if I were in her shoes, I'd wait for the media and the people to glorify him and turn him into a martyr before revealing the truth. It would make the revenge much more satisfying. Remember, Tanisha planned on being alive to see this happen,' Patankar said.

'I'm returning to Mumbai immediately,' Mhatre said and hung up.

He had come to spend the week with his parents in Nashik, as Khan had suggested. It allowed him to get away from the media hype around the Girgaum Shootout, and being with his parents would necessarily mean a break from drinking. He was still not sure he could pull off an extended break on his own.

Mhatre and Oscar had met before they both planned to leave for their respective hometowns. On a whim, Mhatre invited him along. The older man was good company.

'Come on,' Mhatre wheedled. 'My parents will be happy to have you over. And you'll get a change of scenery.'

Oscar thought for a moment, and then smiled his acquiescence.

The days that followed included long conversations over endless cups of tea in the courtyard of Mhatre's ancestral house. Mhatre's father, a retired civic worker, took an immediate liking to Oscar, and his mother was only too happy to have one more person to cook for and then bully him into eating one more bhakri.

Quickly, Mhatre brought Oscar up to speed on all that had recently transpired and what he had learned, while the older man listened in shock.

'I have a call to make,' Mhatre said at the end of his account.

Getting up, he went out into the courtyard and dialled Mehta's number. To his surprise, Mehta picked up the call.

'Why?' was all Mhatre said.

'It's not me, Mr Mhatre ...'

'Don't,' Mhatre flared up. 'Don't fucking insult me. Just tell me why.'

There was silence before Mehta spoke.

'Remember what you said about superheroes, Mr Mhatre?'

'I remember,' Mhatre replied through clenched teeth.

'Not all superheroes are given power. Some have to snatch it. There is so much to be done in this world, for this world. But no one takes notice of you unless there is a tragedy involved. For me, it began when my father died in a fire. I became a hero for all accident victims. With popularity came more business deals, more money. And all of that money, all of it, mind you, I used to build our country's security. Unlike my selfish father, who believed in hoarding it all.'

'Innocent people died at Shivaji Park, you sick motherfucker!'

'They weren't supposed to!' Mehta shouted. 'They were not bloody supposed to! My instructions were clear. I had told Bhatia about that building across the ground which was being razed—I told him the grenade should be thrown there! That stupid bomber Bhatia hired spoiled it all.'

'Oh, no!' Mhatre snapped. 'You don't get to walk away from this so easily. You put the grenade in his hands. A grenade that killed a five-year-old girl!'

'But look at all the good that came of it! The security infrastructure we beefed up! The fame it got you!'

'I did not fucking ask for that fame. And the country did not ask you to engineer a tragedy to "beef up" security. You did this for your own benefit. So say whatever the fuck you like, but we're going to get you, you bastard.'

Mehta was silent for a minute, while Mhatre breathed heavily.

'You'll never be able to prove anything,' Mehta said finally.

'You want to bet? There are enough recorded speeches of yours all over social media. We'll pull samples and compare them with the call. That is, if we don't get one from you. And if you don't give your consent, that will be counted against you in court. And that's just the beginning. I know one very talented woman who will comb through details of thousands of calls made from the location of your house till we find the number you used to call Bhatia. Then we'll find his number. I could go on and on.'

Mehta said nothing.

'Did you hear me? We, as a force, will work together and we will get you. I'm leaving for Mumbai right this minute.'

'And I thought you were a superhero,' Mehta said spitefully. 'Even you don't understand. You're just like the rest of those imbeciles.'

'Maybe, but what *you* are is a cold-blooded killer. And I'll be there to watch when they put a hood over your face and hang you from a rope inside Arthur Road J—'

There was a boom. Then silence.

Mhatre listened to the silence in shock. Then he hung up.

He knew a gunshot when he heard one.

Epilogue

'Sasure pe marti hai, O kudi mere sasure pe marti hai...'

Patankar was in his element, leaning back in his chair and tapping away on his phone.

'Pretty sure some lyricist is going to file a case against you one of these days, sir,' Mhatre said from the door of his cabin.

Patankar looked up happily. He laid his phone on the desk and went over to envelop Mhatre in a warm hug.

'Kaisa hai, gandu?' he asked.

Mhatre burst out laughing and Patankar joined in.

Thanks to Niyaz Ansari's confession, the complaint against Mhatre had been dismissed. The inquiry into his assault on Ansari was still underway, but Ansari had given an official statement saying he did not want Mhatre to face any action for that. The department could not ignore the fact that Mhatre's conduct had been unbecoming for a uniformed personnel, but Khan had taken him aside and told him that he would be dismissing it with a mildly negative remark in his

Annual Confidential Report, and that the positive remarks on it would far outstrip the others in number, and in magnitude.

'Thank you, sir,' Mhatre had said. 'What next?'

'What next?' Khan asked. 'Get to the squad office! Crimes in my zone aren't going to solve themselves.'

Mhatre had saluted Khan and then he rode his bike to the squad office, grinning from ear to ear the whole time.

Kadam had greeted him with a big smile as he walked in. For a brief moment, he considered asking her if she wanted to have dinner after work. Ultimately, he decided against it. She had asked him when she felt like it, and he had turned her down for the sake of his addiction. If she still felt the same way, it was her choice, not his, and he would wait to find out.

Mhatre told Patankar what Khan had said about the enquiry, and Patankar nodded.

'I'd expect nothing less from him,' he said. 'Khan sir might not be everyone's favourite, but he's a good cop and a fair man.'

Mhatre had to agree.

'I'll just catch up on some paperwork, then,' he said, indicating his desk outside Patankar's cabin, which had a huge stack of files and documents on it.

'Go for it. You want to get a drink after work?'

Mhatre hesitated.

Intersections

'Don't think so, sir,' he said finally. 'It's been a good spell of being sober. I'd like to try and keep it going.'

Patankar smiled again.

'In that case, I won't ask you again,' he said. Mhatre nodded gratefully. Recovery from addiction was easier if the environment was conducive, rather than detrimental.

He walked to his desk and settled down. Making sure Kadam's back was turned, he raised both his hands and looked at them. There was no tremor.

He had cleared the first file from the stack when Patankar came out, looking all back-to-business-like.

'A dead body washed ashore at the fishermen's colony in Badhwar Park,' he said. 'Khan sir wants us there.'

Mhatre and Kadam stood up, slipped their cellphones into their pockets and prepared to step out.

At the door, Mhatre paused, turned and ran his eyes around the squad office.

He smiled.

He was home.

Acknowledgements

The biggest share of my gratitude, which, frankly, is limitless and undying, goes to my mother Shubha. This book is a culmination of thirty-four years of upbringing that has literally made me what I am today. It was she who made me fall in love with reading at a very young age, which ultimately led to a passion for writing fiction. None of what I have achieved would have been possible without her. The writing of this book has taken a lot of qualities like persistence, dedication, hard work and discipline, and all of those exist in me because she exists. I could write a separate book and could still not write enough about how much she means to me.

Without doubt or argument, the other person in whose debt I shall forever remain is S. Hussain Zaidi, my mentor, first boss and role model. He taught me a lot about what I do for a living, shaped me as a crime reporter when I began my career under him in *The Asian Age*, circa 2008, roped me in on some of his projects during this time and turned me into a sounding board for his fiction ideas, in the process educating me a lot. Not to mention the daily Urdu lessons and that eternally touching gesture of dedicating his novel, *The Eleventh Hour*, to me. *Huzoor-e-Mualim, hum izhar-e-tashakkur ke liye ta-umr makool aur baligh alfaazon ki qillat mehsoos karte rehange.*

Heartfelt thanks to my editor Suresh Nambath, resident editor Vikas Dhoot and city editor Aditya Anand at *The Hindu* for supporting me in this endeavour and making it possible for me to pursue my dream along with my career. Adi has been a friend before he became my boss, and I have a lot to thank him for when it comes to this book, including asking him random questions based on my wild ideas late at night after work.

A huge thank you to Jaspinder Kang at Golden Pen for the opportunity, to Jenil Parmar for helping me deal with the technicalities and the paperwork, which I am horrible at, and Mradula Mahajan, who, with timely reminders, subtly but firmly let me know that the clock was ticking.

In one of the chapters, PI Sharad Patankar tells Mhatre that 'hindsight is a luxury only available to those on the sidelines'. That statement was actually made in a television news debate by the late Himanshu Roy, an IPS officer who, in the formative years of my career, guided and helped me no end. I sincerely wish he were here today to see this book being released.

I already know what he would have said to me. That one line in the book is but a small tribute to Roy sir.

This book would never have been complete without the skilful and efficient editing by the Westland team and the fabulous cover art by Gavin Morris. You are the absolute best.

A lot of crime investigation techniques described in this book are the result of lengthy conversations with scores of police officers that I have got to know over the course of my career. Although they wish to remain nameless, they know who they are, and I would like to let them know that their help has been invaluable to me.

It would hardly take an ace investigator to guess that this book is based on my observations and experiences as a crime reporter. In the eleven-odd years that I have been on the crime beat, I have had the good fortune of observing both policemen and policing up close.

Perhaps like everyone else on the beat, I entered the profession with a completely different picture of the police force in my mind, one filled with car chases and tense stand-offs between armed men and brutal interrogations in dark lock-ups. The fact that I inadvertently walked in on a live interrogation in one corner of a suburban police station on my very first day on the job did nothing to help the situation.

It took me months, perhaps years, to realise that real policing can be very tedious, and at times even boring. The average policeman spends hours of his professional life filling out paperwork or on patrol duty so boring and monotonous that it can hardly be described in words. But it is this very monotony that builds the foundation of a strong career. The countless hours spent pounding the pavement lead to the building of a source network that, to a large extent, is the very basis of crime investigation.

A lot of people ask me if reporting the crime beat is challenging. I tell them that it is literally the simplest beat in journalism. If my time on the job has taught me one thing beyond doubt, it is that anyone, and I mean anyone, is capable of committing a crime. Hence, policing, and to an extent crime reporting, is a study of basic human nature.

The purpose behind this novel is manifold. Firstly, it is to stay true to the first form of writing that I fell in love with—fiction writing. This, again, is thanks in no small part to my mother, who instilled the love for reading in me from a very young age. From getting lost in stories written by others to writing my own by the time I started college has been a wonderful journey.

It has taken years of disagreements with janaab Zaidi saahab, but I have finally convinced him to let me write fiction as opposed to non-fiction, which is a genre he favours over others. Creating entire worlds within the confines of an MS Word document is a high in itself and one that I am not sure I can ever live without.

The other purpose is to present a more accurate depiction of policing and crime detection, which I have had the privilege of studying more closely than a lot of others. Ever in support of those who do not get their due, I have purposely steered clear of centring the story around the two over-used ranks of policemen in popular culture—inspector and sub-inspector. The protagonist of my story is an API, an assistant police inspector, which is a rank right in the middle. Not too new and junior, not too jaded and old. Just a middle level cop who, I think, should get his due as well.

Finally, my sincere apologies for all those whose favourite songs I have ruined through Patankar's character. If it helps, *O Hansini* is one of my personal favourites and it took a great deal of effort to ruin it.